THE
COWBOY'S
Romantic Dreamer

VALERIE COMER

Valerie Comer Bibliography

Urban Farm Fresh Romance

0. Promise of Peppermint (ebook only)
1. Secrets of Sunbeams
2. Butterflies on Breezes
3. Memories of Mist
4. Wishes on Wildflowers
5. Flavors of Forever
6. Raindrops on Radishes
7. Dancing at Daybreak

Saddle Springs Romance

1. The Cowboy's Christmas Reunion
2. The Cowboy's Mixed-Up Matchmaker
3. The Cowboy's Romantic Dreamer
4. The Cowboy's Convenient Marriage

Christmas in Montana Romance

1. More Than a Tiara
2. Other Than a Halo
3. Better Than a Crown

Garden Grown Romance
(Arcadia Valley Romance)

1. Sown in Love (ebook only)
2. Sprouts of Love
3. Rooted in Love
4. Harvest of Love

Farm Fresh Romance

1. Raspberries and Vinegar
2. Wild Mint Tea
3. Sweetened with Honey
4. Dandelions for Dinner
5. Plum Upside Down
6. Berry on Top

Riverbend Romance Novellas

1. Secretly Yours
2. Pinky Promise
3. Sweet Serenade
4. Team Bride
5. Merry Kisses

valeriecomer.com/books

Trevor Delgado liked all these people just fine, but when those two women started looking at each other that way, it made a guy nervous. They were creating a talent show. That should definitely let him off the hook, since he had no talents.

His knee jittered, but he readied himself to shake his head. *Ready, set, no.*

Lauren Carmichael and Denae Archibald weren't up on the meaning of *no*. They just figured a guy probably didn't understand enough to say *yes*. Any objections could be overcome.

They were wrong. He'd hold out.

Denae turned to Cheri. "Would you be interested in donating a painting?"

Trevor's sister-in-law, Cheri, rubbed her hands across her round belly. "Probably. So long as this little one is patient about his or her arrival."

"The event isn't until the end of May, so you've got

lots of time." Lauren made a note on her tablet. "The baby's due in, what, ten weeks?"

"About that. May third."

He tried to ignore his brother's arm slipping around Cheri's shoulder and tugging her close. Refused to notice the smile they shared. He was happy for Kade. Really, he was. The guy was such a sap it was hard not to cheer him on. Kade had been in love with Cheri since they were teens, and they'd reunited a year ago. This baby would make three kids, rounding out his and hers with — finally — theirs. A convoluted path, but it had ended in happily-ever-after all the same.

Trevor wasn't used to thinking in terms of that phrase, but Denae Archibald's re-entry into their group had expanded his vocabulary. She was a freelance romance editor, more than willing to explain the ins and outs of character arcs and plot points to whomever would listen. Anyone who knew so much about romance ought to be happily married herself by now, but Denae was still on the manhunt.

Reason enough for Trevor to keep a low profile, not that she had designs on him. Like, who would? Of the three Delgado brothers, he was the eldest, the loner, the one too absorbed in riding the western Montana ranges to have a social life. He'd had a chance or two at relationships a few years back, blown it, and was going to stay a bachelor until he died.

Denae beamed at Cheri, her whole face lit by that megawatt smile, as though her friend's pregnancy was her personal joy in life. Course, she was probably the most happy and gorgeous person Trevor knew. Her sparkly eyes about drove him crazy. She was different from all the girls he'd grown up with, an unknown entity. One he clearly needed to keep an eye on lest she rope him into something he'd later regret.

"We have you and Garret down for music."

Trevor's head jerked before he could control it. Before he saw Denae looking pointedly at James. Whew.

The other guys exchanged a glance and a shrug. "Sure."

"A solo, Kade?"

Kade furrowed his brow. "I don't know. I haven't done any public singing in quite a while."

Here it came. Trevor planted his feet deeper into the plush area rug in front of the leather sofa, trying to keep his knee from jiggling. What should he do with his hands? Why wasn't he holding a mug to give them something to do?

"Maybe with Trev." Lauren's voice. "I haven't heard you two sing together in years."

"No." There. He'd gotten the word out. Now he simply had to stick to it against a stampede of yearling calves.

Denae's long black hair swung as she turned to face him. "You sing?"

"No."

"You used to," countered Lauren.

"Not anymore."

Denae frowned. "How can you just stop?"

"He hit puberty in front of the congregation on a Sunday morning." Kade chuckled. "We were singing a duet — what was it, Trev, Rock of Ages? — and his voice went all over the place. Up, squeak, down, squeak. It was hilarious."

"It wasn't funny," Trevor ground out. "Not even a little bit."

"Oh, man, it was, too. You need to learn to laugh at yourself."

Not happening. He raised his eyebrows and looked between Denae and Lauren. "To make a long story short, I'm not participating in your talent show. I also don't build stuff to donate to the auction. It's a great charity, so I'll come. I'll bid on things. I'll heckle the participants, especially if one of them is my kid brother. But I'm not performing."

"Well, thanks." Kade laughed. "Not sure I can handle being up front without my big bro." He turned to Denae. "I'll think about it and see if I come up with anything. How secular an event is this? I mean, would it be okay to do a Christian song?"

"I don't see why not. It's family-friendly, so there are strictures against foul language and the like, but no one on the council said anything about religious content."

Across the room, Garret picked at a piece of fluff from the area rug where he sat cross-legged. "How come you're on the arts council anyway, Denae? I didn't know you were an artist."

Trevor hadn't known that, either. Plus, he rather liked someone else being in the hot seat for a moment. It sure beat being picked on for a cracking adolescent voice. Having a chance to watch Denae without anyone noticing was also a great benefit.

His hands stilled on his thighs.

Really? No way. He was only a little curious about her. That was all. There might be plenty of room in his house, but there wasn't room in his heart or life for a woman. They were too unpredictable.

Look at Cheri. She'd run off a week before her wedding to Kade, leaving his brother heartbroken. Yeah, they'd eventually reunited, but only after a lot of pain. Watching his brother's despair had nearly killed Trevor.

Look at Lauren. She said she'd loved James since they were teens, but wasn't pushing him off on other women for years a strange way to show it? Yeah, okay, they'd finally admitted their mutual adoration and been married last Christmas, but was the decade of agony worth it?

Trevor didn't do pain. He didn't do does-she-love-me-or-not games. He'd dabbled in that one once, gotten burned, and learned his lesson. He wasn't stupid enough to blindly go back for more, even if a different woman dealt the cards this time.

Nope.

"—amazing!" came Lauren's voice. "Show them, Denae."

Oh. He'd missed the announcement.

Denae glanced at him — why him? — and hesitated.

He forced out a casual grin. She didn't affect him. He wouldn't let her. "Sure. Show us." Then he could clue into what he'd missed. A guy needed to know what his friends were up to.

She could be his friend. They hung out in the same crowd, after all. They were more Kade's gang than his, typical of their entire lives when his little brother gathered friends like the Pied Piper, and Trevor tagged along. It had been easier than finding his own, with a mere eighteen months separating them. Only one grade apart in school.

Cheri stretched a hand toward Denae as though they could touch across the room. "Go ahead."

"Yeah, Denae." Garret nodded. "If you can do it at the talent show, there's nothing to fear from us."

Trevor narrowed his gaze at Garret. Was the ranchland newcomer making a play for Denae? That would be good, right? Because Trevor wasn't getting involved with anyone. Still, thinking 'Go, Garret' immediately morphed to 'Go away, Garret.'

Yeah. This was going to be a problem.

WHY DIDN'T Trevor's face reveal anything?

Denae Archibald didn't let her gaze linger on the strong, silent oldest member of this group that had welcomed her in. She didn't need to stare at him to remember every plane of his angular face, every dip of the thick brows that shaded his dark eyes, the ever-present five o'clock shadow.

He was gorgeous enough to take her breath away, and he'd done so every time she'd seen him in the past ten months since she'd moved back to Saddle Springs where Dad and his second wife had owned a ranch when she was a kid. She'd loved summers at Standing Rock, loved riding wild and free in the mountains, away from her creeper stepdad and bratty little half-brothers. Dad had sold that ranch to the Delgado family a few years ago and simply told Denae after the fact, as though it wouldn't matter that he'd ripped away her happy place. He'd thought nothing of it, had no clue what the ranch meant to her.

Now Trevor Delgado lived alone in the magnificent ranch house she loved so much. Which was worse, imagining this particular man sprawled in front of one of the field-rock fireplaces, or imagining the stately home with only one person in it?

Sometimes she thought he watched her in an interested sort of way but, if so, why didn't he make a move? She was a pure romantic, old-fashioned enough to think the guy should express interest first but, one of these days, she just might take matters into her own hands come what may.

Denae fumbled with her tablet until she found the portfolio she was looking for then handed it to Garret on her left without a word.

"Scroll through it," suggested Lauren. The friend who'd been with Denae through thick and thin since the move and even before.

Garret emitted a low whistle and glanced at Denae with an approving nod. "Nice work." He handed the tablet to Carmen, who handed it to Cheri, who handed it to Kade, who handed it to Trevor.

Denae held her breath. Would he see what she'd tried to capture in those photos? The essence of people's souls through their eyes, the beauty of each face, each body, even though not perfect by society's standards? What she wouldn't give to photograph Trevor. She'd shoot him outdoors, on his black gelding, that cowboy hat in place. She'd capture those dark, mysterious eyes.

The ones that looked at her now. Really looked at her, as though a piece of the photographer had found its way through the subjects and on to the viewer.

He dipped his head. "Definitely a talent." He passed the tablet to James's sister Tori who sat on the floor nearby, but he still studied Denae.

She was caught. Couldn't avert her gaze. All she could do was try to convey, somehow, that she was as aware of him as he seemed to be of her at that moment in time. *Ask me out, Trevor.* Could she beg that with her eyes without anyone else noticing?

He looked away, the connection severed.

"Do you do family sittings?" asked Cheri. "I've been after my in-laws to get new portraits done. We should update the Eaglecrest website, too."

Family sittings? Not usually, but if it meant getting Trevor in front of the lens, it might be worth it. "I'm sure we can work something out. Do you want to do it before or after the baby?"

Cheri's hand went to her belly. "I hadn't thought that far. Probably after, when spring has come to the ranch and the apple trees are in blossom."

Kade caressed Cheri's shoulder. "We'll have to schedule around Sawyer if we're doing family photos."

Right, the youngest Delgado. The rodeo cowboy who was rarely home. A guy who risked life and limb for an instant of glory held no interest for Denae. Not when there were men like Trevor who worked hard every day, regardless of the weather, regardless of the praise, regardless of the loneliness.

Because a person couldn't spend so much time alone without being lonely, right? Denae would go nuts without people around. Her chosen career as a romance novel editor was solitary enough, even though she entered romantic, flower-strewn worlds where devoted couples overcame all odds to find their true love. Still, when she closed a manuscript, she found herself back in the tiny spare bedroom of her rented duplex with Poppy's big brown puppy-dog eyes looking up at her.

Still without a love of her own.

CHAPTER 2

Bro, you've got talent. Remember Jesus said not to dig a hole and bury what He's given us."

Trevor lifted two cookies from the tray on the kitchen island and turned to Kade, who'd managed to sneak up behind him. Cheri and Lauren, holding teacups, leaned against the far counter, chatting. The others were still in the great room. "A safe house for abused women is a good cause. I'll donate."

"You're missing the point."

No, he got the point just fine, but that wasn't enough to nudge him out of his comfort zone. "I'm too rusty at anything I ever dabbled in to call it talent. Pretty sure they're not looking for calf roping. 'Cause I'm good at that. Not that I've tried it on the community hall stage."

Kade chuckled.

Whew. Situation diverted.

"You might be rusty, but three months is plenty of time to brush up your skills. Sing with me? We can go with one of the old hymns, a newer worship song, a folk song... you pick."

His brother could be so stubborn, but they shared genetics, so Trevor could out-stubborn him. "Which part of no did you not understand? The n? Or was it the o?"

"Oh, I've got a three-year-old who says it often enough I haven't forgotten its meaning, trust me." Kade's face grew serious. "Worried about you, bro."

"No need."

"Look, I get that you're more of an introvert than I am, but don't even introverts need a life?"

Trevor shrugged. "Hey, I'm here, aren't I? Lauren called a meeting, and I showed up. I can't help it all you old married folk are too busy to get together with the gang as often as you used to. Besides, there's no shortage of work on the ranch regardless of the time of year. As you know."

"I know. When we're not hauling hay for the cows, we're keeping the horses exercised. But I wouldn't have it any other way."

Neither would Trevor, except for the fact that his brother came home to a wife and two kids after he'd put in his hours at the ranch headquarters. Trevor, on the other hand, went home to a silent mansion with a container of leftovers packed by his parents' cook.

How could his brother take a chance on love, not once, but three times, and come out so happy? Trevor longed to take the leap, but he wouldn't. Kade might've landed in a pleasant place, but Trevor wouldn't be so lucky. He'd crash and burn. Again.

"I'm not giving up on you." Kade's voice brought

Trevor back to the moment. "I've heard you sing in church. I know you've got a great voice, and I want to sing with you again."

Trevor opened his mouth to reply, but Kade's hand silenced him. "Whatever you're afraid of isn't going to happen, bro."

Applause. That's what he was afraid of. Being in the spotlight, all eyes on him. He shook his head. "You can present all the logic you want, but it won't make a difference."

Kade's eyes searched his.

Trevor looked away, lest his little brother see more than he wanted him to. But he didn't want to watch Denae and Carmen enter the kitchen, either, chatting like two magpies. Only with sweeter voices. He lifted a cookie. "These are good. Cheri make them?"

"She and the kids, yes. Can't you tell by the uneven shapes that Jericho was helping?"

Trevor chuckled. The treats were definitely multi-sized and oddly shaped. He bit off half a cookie. "Doesn't hurt the flavor any."

"Thing is, he won't get better at it if he doesn't get practice."

"Would you let up already?"

Kade angled his head, those dark brown eyes drilling Trevor's. "Nope. Embrace life, bro."

"I'm not like you and Sawyer. I'm not a risk-taker."

"Just being alive is a risk. And that parable Jesus told of the rich man who gave his servants talents and told them to use them wisely?"

"Yeah, yeah, I know." Trevor's conscience bit hard. "The servants who invested gained rewards."

"And the one who buried his talent definitely didn't." Kade nudged his shoulder against Trevor's. "Think on it." He wandered over to where the four women had gathered, wrapped an arm around Cheri's expanding waist, and nuzzled her neck.

Trevor swallowed his envy. His kid brother was right. Nothing big ever happened without someone sticking his neck out.

Denae laughed at something Cheri said then her gaze slid past the others and locked on Trevor's like a lasso tightening around a calf's neck. Down for the count.

Time stood still until he managed to wrench his focus away and toss the rest of the cookie in his mouth. There was no way her look meant anything. She wasn't his type and, for sure, he wasn't hers. Imagine how exhausting it would be to hang around with a social butterfly. To listen to incessant chatter.

Imagine how bored she'd be with him in ten minutes flat. He was no life of the party. Give him a horse and the great outdoors any day of the week. Give him stock to feed and stalls to clean. Give him an alfalfa field coming into bloom, ready to cut and bale for hay.

"Trevor?"

He stilled then slowly turned toward her. She was tall, her head coming past his shoulder. He wouldn't have to bend far to kiss her. He'd shift that long black hair over her shoulders, put his hands around her thin waist, and...

Trevor took a step back and slammed into the

counter. Definitely one of his stupider thoughts, which took some doing. He was the master of them. "Yeah?"

"I wasn't trying to put you on the spot."

"Uh... it's okay." Was it hot in here, or what?

"I was just hoping everyone would be able to think of some way to contribute. If not a performance for the event, then maybe an item for the silent auction. A safe house for women in abusive situations is such a good cause. There are women even in a small community like this who need those services."

"Definitely a good cause. I... uh, I could make a donation. I mean, that's what the whole thing is about, right? Raising funds? I'll cut straight to the chase and write a check."

"Where's the fun in that?" She brushed her thick bangs to one side.

His gaze snapped back to her laughing eyes. "Not everything's about fun. Sometimes it's about getting things done."

Her fingers rested on his forearm, branding and searing him to the core. He couldn't draw a breath to save his life, not with his vision filled with her pretty brown eyes, his senses filled with her floral scent, his ears filled with her teasing voice.

What had they been talking about again? Trevor shifted sideways along the counter until Denae's hand fell away. "I've got to go."

"Promise you'll think about it?" Her eyes widened as she smiled.

"Sure, but I honestly don't have any useful skills, so the answer will still be no. We're starting into one of the busiest seasons on the ranch, too, with calving starting soon. I just can't. Excuse me, please." He dodged around her and headed for the foyer where his parka, boots, and cowboy hat awaited him. He pressed the remote starter on his truck — anything to save a few seconds of his escape.

A minute later he slid into the cab, which hadn't had time to warm up even one degree. He flicked the wipers, dislodging the half inch of soft snow that had fallen while he'd been inside, and shifted into drive.

A large, silent house awaited him. He'd start a blaze in one of the fireplaces, put on some music, and immerse himself in his research of a new crop for the tired hayfields belonging to Cheri's grandparents, now controlled by the Delgado family.

Better than thinking about Denae. Or talents.

Or what might have been with Meg.

DENAE SLID into the backseat of Lauren and James's Jeep Wrangler. Her friends had driven right through Saddle Springs on their way to Cheri and Kade's new house anyway, so they'd offered her a ride.

Lauren turned in her seat as James brushed the accumulated snow off the vehicle. "That went pretty well, didn't it?"

"I think so. What's Trevor's story all about?"

"I don't know, honestly. He was a lot more fun back in high school, but by the time I came back to town with my veterinary degree, he'd turned into this hermit. I was gone for eight years, mind you, and the grapevine doesn't work as well as you'd think."

Denae laughed. "Good to know the reputation of small-town gossip isn't always warranted." Still, she was dying to know what caused Trevor's reserve. It couldn't all be from that one Sunday morning in his adolescence, could it? No, not if he was still fun in high school.

Not for the first time, she wished she'd pushed to live with her dad through her teens instead of getting sucked into staying in Cannon Beach with Mom. It wasn't like she could protect her mother from Mark. She'd barely been able to protect herself. But her life had been full with a summer job at a bookstore, babysitting her young half-brothers, and hanging out with her best friend, Sadie. Thoughts of the ranch in western Montana had dimmed as time went on.

Cannon Beach without Mark would have been great. She loved the ocean, but the mountains and rangeland and rivers fed her soul in a deeper way. She'd come home, plain and simple... except that it wasn't quite home since Dad had sold the ranch.

James slid into the driver's seat and smacked his gloved hands together. "Cold out there."

"It *is* still winter." Lauren laughed.

"Yep, and I'm ready for spring." He inched the Jeep down the steep driveway, following Trevor's tracks.

"You were in Saddle Springs when I was away for school." Lauren eyed James. "What happened to Trevor?"

James shot her a glance as he shrugged. "No idea. He's always hung around the gang more because of Kade than anyone else, I think. I can't remember ever having a deep one-on-one with him."

Men. Seriously. "Who's his best friend?"

James met Denae's gaze in the rearview mirror. "Dunno. Kade, probably. Why?"

"Because everyone needs someone."

He laughed as he turned left at the end of the driveway, while Trevor's tracks went the other way. "Guys aren't the same as girls. Besides the obvious, you know..."

She could make him elaborate, but she wasn't quite that mean. "I get that, but last I heard, members of the male species were still humans, and humans need community. Granted, some need it more than others."

"Trevor doesn't seem to. I don't know. Worrying about him hasn't kept me awake at night."

Denae rolled her eyes. Obviously Lauren and James weren't the right people to ask, but Cheri might be too close to Trevor. Or she'd tell her husband about Denae's curiosity, and Kade would tell Trevor. Nope. Not going there.

"Those are good photos you took." James steered around the hairpin turn as they wound down River Road. "You've got a knack for capturing beneath the surface."

Denae bit her lip. "Thanks." She'd worked hard on that, capturing the essence of the women she photographed. Everyone had beauty, whether they could see it themselves or not. Whether they were obese or anorexic or struggling with self-worth in some other way.

Her project had started with her own journey from anorexia, with her self-portraits. Seeing the pilgrimage through the viewfinder had encouraged her to offer that service to others, like her friend Sadie, whose struggle had been the opposite of Denae's. She'd come a long way in the past year or two, though, shedding not only a lot of weight but many insecurities along the way. And she'd married a great guy last fall, a mere few weeks before Lauren and James's wedding.

At twenty-eight, Denae should expect her friends to be pairing up. Some friends from Cannon Beach were already on their second marriages. She was holding out for true, lasting love — not serial monogamy — but her patience was wearing thin. Her guy had to be out there somewhere. She'd been so sure she'd find him in Saddle Springs, tipping his cowboy hat at her.

It wasn't going to be Garret Morrison, whose puppy-dog eyes reminded her of her springer spaniel's. It wasn't going to be Sawyer Delgado or Dillon Scarborough or Bryce Sutherland. If it wasn't Trevor Delgado, maybe she'd give in to Sadie's begging and move to Spokane. Surely a city that size had enough single men she could find her Mr. Right.

But first, she'd give Trevor more time. And maybe just a wee nudge or two to get things rolling.

CHAPTER 3

Did he have any talents?

The question shimmered in front of Trevor's eyes, refusing to let him focus on crop research. He pushed the keyboard away, wandered into the kitchen, and set a kettle of water to boil.

Beyond the breakfast room windows, falling snow swirled in the lights by the back door. He and the two dogs would brave the elements one more time to check on the horses before he called it a night.

That wasn't a talent. That was simply being a responsible man.

Of course, everyone had talents. Maybe not the kind a guy could perform in front of a crowd, but something. Trevor was adept at riding, at cutting the herd, at roping calves. Not good enough to ride rodeo like Sawyer, but he didn't want that life, anyway.

He was good at the business end of things. He'd taken courses at the community college and gone on to get his degree online. He still took courses in agriculture, because there was always something to learn.

He and Dad spent hours fine-tuning the direction for the entire Eaglecrest operation. With the addition of Standing Rock several years ago and now managing Cheri's family spread, Paradise Creek, there was a lot to consider. A lot to keep on top of. The Delgados did so well because they were forward thinkers, and it didn't hurt that Trevor's three-times-great-grandfather had been one of the earliest ranchers in the area, securing a large spread and beginning to build the Delgado reputation.

Trevor turned back to the kitchen, dropped a teabag into a giant pottery mug, and poured boiling water over it. He hadn't given the former owners a passing thought in the first couple of years he'd lived in this house. Since Denae had moved back to Saddle Springs, he'd increasingly visualized her in his kitchen. That was only because she'd stayed with Stewy and Michelle often as a kid, so she'd known this house well.

All of it. Whereas Trevor never ascended to the second floor. Why bother, when the master suite was on the main? Mom sent Elnora over to dust the four bedrooms up there every couple of months. Good enough. Even on the first floor, Trevor kept the pocket doors to the formal living and dining rooms closed. He also didn't bother with the study, but had set up his office area in the family room. There was still at least twice too much space for one guy.

Talents. He was good at compartmentalizing his life.

Before he could think too hard or long, he strode down the short hallway to the master bedroom and into the gigantic walk-in closet. A few boxes of childhood memorabilia sat in one corner. Trevor dug into the bottom one and withdrew the 1/2-size violin case.

He hadn't touched that thing since he was eight. Since Sawyer had jumped off the top bunk and snapped the bow.

Trevor unlatched the case and stroked the violin's spruce body and rosewood fingerboard. He picked it up and tightened the strings with trembling fingers. It was so tiny under his chin, and his fingers were too thick for the string spacing.

The bow was still broken.

Mom had scolded Sawyer and offered to pick up a new one next time she was in Missoula, but Trevor had shrugged it off. He'd insisted it didn't matter, that he was too big to waste time on baby stuff, that he had puppies to play with and a pony to ride.

Why had he done that? Why had he severed the one thing that made him different from his brothers?

Because it made him different. Because *Kade* didn't want violin lessons, or piano, or guitar, or anything else. Because rough-and-tumble little cowpokes played hard outside all day and fell asleep covered in dust with their spurred boots still on their feet.

Trevor plucked the strings, their sound sweetly resonating after all these years. Sure, it needed tuning. It needed a bow. And, no matter what, it was way too small.

Next time he was in Missoula, he'd buy himself a new one, full size. He'd sign up for online classes or learn off YouTube. No one would ever have to know he'd picked it back up.

He froze, staring at the child-sized instrument in his hands. Why did it still matter? Why couldn't he just be Trevor Russell Delgado, a cowboy who played music?

It wasn't like his parents would frown. Great-granddad Donovan had fiddled for dances and fairs across the region. Music was part of the Delgado fiber.

Then what was his hang-up? His memory shot straight back to that horrific Sunday when his voice broke, not once, but several times before he'd given up. He couldn't even remember if Kade finished the song without him. He'd dashed off the platform and hidden behind the baptismal until Dad found him long after the service had ended and everyone else had gone home.

The memories were intertwined.

No, they weren't. Trevor shook his head. Sawyer had broken his bow at least five years before that. It hadn't been the same time period at all. Why was his head so messed up?

Where had all his confidence gone? In music. In romance. In life.

He remembered the desperation with which he'd pursued Meg Carmichael. Meg, several years younger, had gone wild in high school, without a care in the world what anyone thought of her. If she felt like doing it, she did it. Didn't matter if she left a string of guys high and dry, and she had. Didn't matter if she broke her parents' hearts, and she had. Didn't matter if she thumbed her nose at God, and she had.

What had been so attractive about Meg? That devil-may-care attitude had been the polar opposite of straight-laced Trevor Delgado. He should have been disgusted by her. Shunned her. Instead, he'd admired her and been just a little jealous.

He passed the quarter-century mark as the perfect son while in love with Meg. Kade had already been jilted. Sawyer had bailed out of Saddle Springs pursuing rodeo trophies the minute he'd graduated from Mustang County High. And the steady-as-a-rock oldest son debated tossing everything to the wind.

He and Meg had been good together. He'd kept their relationship a secret, slow to give in to her demands, weighing everything constantly. She'd thought of him as a challenge, sure she could bring him into line. A little more time, and Trevor had no doubt she would've succeeded, but then she'd become pregnant.

Trevor stepped away, washing his hands of her. He knew for a fact the baby wasn't his — he'd kept his jeans zipped — but living without Meg stabbed him. Knowing he wasn't her one-and-only twisted the dagger. Even so, if she'd twitched a finger to beckon him closer, he would've gone.

He knew it.

He wasn't proud of it.

But when she'd done an about-face a couple of years later, he'd missed his chance. She'd forsaken her lifestyle and married Eli Thornton, who'd taken on little Aiden like he was the boy's biological dad. And last summer, they'd had a baby girl.

By all accounts, Meg and Eli were deliriously happy.

And that was great. Really. But where did it leave Trevor? Surely it was time he set aside his dreams of what-might-have-been and focused on his own future, like Meg had done.

The thought terrified him. He was obviously a bad judge of character. No, that wasn't entirely true. He'd known Meg was a poor choice, but his heart hadn't cared one teensy speck. How could he trust himself the next time?

It was simply easiest if there wasn't a next time.

Ever.

DENAE SCANNED through Track Changes then clicked to save and close the document. She halted her treadmill before linking her hands and stretching them above her head and from side to side.

That had been such a sweet story, and it would be so much stronger if the author took Denae's suggestions to heart. Denae almost hated sending this one back. It was the final in a series about five brothers, all alpha males. That part might be a bit unrealistic — how much coursing testosterone could one family handle? — but the author had pulled it off.

No doubt about it, the romance genre thrived on big, bad, strong heroes. Only a few authors, like that chick Valerie Comer, wrote believable and adorable beta heroes. Oh, and Elizabeth Maddrey. A couple of others, maybe.

Where were the men like Trevor Delgado? The macho men who held back, a strange combo of alpha and... shy? What made a guy like Trevor tick? If only an author sent her a story to edit about a hero with his characteristics, it would give her some ideas.

Reading hundreds — maybe thousands — of romances had schooled Denae to believe the right man was out there waiting to sweep her off her feet.

The only thing Trevor swept was the stable and probably his kitchen floor. Not that she knew for sure... but there didn't seem to be a trail of broken hearts behind him.

Why? He was a solid hunk of a man. Tall, lean, and gorgeous. Rippling muscles. Strong and silent, but fun, too, when he loosened up a little. Devoted to his family. Hard working... seriously, what was not to love?

If she couldn't formulate a plan going forward from all the romance she'd read and edited, she'd have to wing it. What was the way to a man's heart?

His stomach, said the old adage. First problem, Trevor had a rancher's steak-and-potatoes appetite, whereas Denae lived on salads. Yes, she was trying to get over herself and eat appropriately, enough to keep a human functioning, not just a songbird.

Poppy stretched from her mat on the floor, her stub of a tail wagging.

"Hey, pretty girl." Denae squatted and wrapped her arms around the liver-and-white spaniel, who proceeded to lick her cheek. At least somebody loved her. Denae giggled as she buried her fingers in the soft coat. "Want to go for a run?" If running were even a possibility in the deep, fresh snow.

Poppy wiggled out of Denae's arms, trotted to the top of the narrow staircase, and looked back expectantly.

"Okay, let's go." Downstairs, Denae quickly bunched her long hair into a ponytail and tied on her waterproof joggers. Gaiters to keep her lower legs dry. Headband, light down parka, gloves. Check. She snagged Poppy's lead from the hook by the front door and snapped it in place.

Outside, white snow sparkled in the sunlight, and the temperature was probably ten degrees warmer than she'd expected. Her spirits lifted. This sure beat the winter gloom of coastal Oregon. Poppy trotting at her side, she jogged down the middle of Clark Avenue, since no one had shoveled the sidewalks and there was no traffic in sight.

Except the SUV that had just rounded the curve a few blocks away. As it drew near, Denae guided Poppy to the side in shin-deep snow and waited for it to pass.

Instead, the driver's window rolled down and Carmen Haviland leaned out. "Denae! You're a diehard jogger. I had no idea."

"Poppy doesn't care what the weather is. When she needs to go out, she needs to go out. Besides, isn't it gorgeous? Much too perfect to stay cooped up. You must think so yourself."

Carmen laughed. "You got me there, only I'm in town to pick Uncle Howard up from the hospital. He had an ugly gut infection and became dehydrated, so they admitted him a couple of days ago. But, today he's cleared to come home, so it doesn't matter how much it snowed. Even waiting the half hour for Juliana and me to get down from the ranch is killing him."

"You're so good to him." The old man wasn't even

Carmen's own uncle, but the great-uncle of her deceased husband.

"Aw, he's pretty tender underneath that crusty exterior. Like a perfect loaf of sourdough bread."

Denae managed a grin, but the comparison was pretty much lost. When was the last time she'd eaten bread? Ages ago. That many calories and carbs needed major benefits... and didn't have them. Instead of responding, she tapped on the rear window and peeked at five-year-old Juliana.

The little girl beamed back.

"Hey, question for you." Carmen's comment returned Denae's attention to the child's mother. "This might be a bit personal, but do you have any plans for Valentine's Day?"

Ugh. The ultimate day of romance. The ultimate day of misery for single people. "I wish I did!" Maybe Trevor would come through yet. He had a couple of days. But, in all honesty, what was the likelihood? Slim to none. Denae shoved the thought away. "Do you have anything in mind?"

"Come out to the Rocking H? We can make pizza and have a girls' night in. Do each others' nails. Facials. A movie. What do you say?"

"I say that sounds a whole lot better than sitting home by myself. If I'm driving out, though, let me bring dinner."

"Aw, no, making the pizza ourselves is half the fun. Bring whatever toppings you'd like that I might not have thought of, though."

"Pepperoni!" called Juliana from the back.

Carmen glanced over her shoulder, smiling. "Don't worry. I've already got the pepperoni."

"That works. Sounds like fun. Are you inviting anyone else?"

"Not sure. I was thinking it might be fun to get to know each other."

With Lauren married and living out at the Flying Horseshoe, Denae could use another friend. A single friend, even if their situations were vastly different. She met Carmen's gaze. "I'd like that."

"Mom..." came Juliana's whine.

"And we need to get going now. We're stopping by Manahan's then picking up Uncle Howard. He's probably pacing the corridors driving the nurses crazy, but not as crazy as he'd make me if I had to take him in with me for groceries."

Denae stepped away from the SUV, Poppy at her side. "Stay in touch!"

"I will." Carmen's window slid up as she waved then pulled away.

CHAPTER 4

I'm so glad you could make it!" Carmen held the door to the old ranch house wide.

"Me, too. I'm also glad it didn't snow anymore this week and that the plows have been up Clark Road."

Carmen chuckled as Denae came in. "That's not a given, for sure. There are too many mountain roads in Mustang County for all of them to be top priority, but Uncle Howard insisted on firing up the old John Deere and clearing our driveway."

"He did a good job." Denae set her bag of salad and a bottle of low-cal dressing on the slate entry floor then tugged off her boots.

"What's this for? I told you I had food covered."

"Just in case." Denae cringed inside. She could do one slice of pizza, right? And then salad. She'd make sure tomorrow was a low-calorie day to make up for it. Her best friend, Sadie, had lost a lot of weight in the past eight months by following Trim Healthy Mama with the help of a personal coach. But Denae had looked into it on her own and discovered a few new recipes for foods both low in fat and low in carbs. Some of them tasted so decadent she didn't quite trust she wouldn't balloon out from eating them, but so far, so good.

Pizza was not on that list.

Then again, Carmen looked an average weight. Definitely not fat, but not as thin as Denae, either. She'd been told she was too skinny. In her head, she knew it was true. In the mirror, she wasn't so sure. Besides, five pounds could easily lead to twenty. She needed to stay in control.

Denae hung her jacket and turned to Carmen with a smile. "What can I say? I love salad, and that's my favorite dressing. I wasn't sure what you had in the house, so I brought my own. No biggie."

By Carmen's raised eyebrows, she wasn't convinced.

"Who's at the door?" came Howard Haviland's booming voice.

"My friend Denae. Remember I told you she was coming?"

The old man appeared in the doorway, sharp eyes piercing Denae. "Right, right. I hope you feed her up good. There's nothing to her. Women need a love handle or two." He guffawed as though it were the funniest joke ever.

She froze. What did he mean by that? She knew what it meant when Mark said it.

Carmen's gaze shifted between them. "Don't mind him. He doesn't notice or care how he comes across."

Denae forced a smile. She'd give him the benefit of the doubt, but she'd keep an eye on him at the same time.

"I'm glad you're feeling better, Mr. Haviland. I'm sure the hospital was no fun."

He sobered, staring at her again. "Full of people sick and dying. I was lucky to get out of there alive."

Was he serious, or was this his attempt at humor? Hard to tell.

Juliana skidded around the corner on her sock feet. "Miss Denae! Come, let's make pizza. Mommy was waiting for you to get here, and I'm so, so hungry."

Grateful for escape, Denae followed the little girl into the farmhouse-style kitchen. No granite-topped island in this one, just two walls of plywood cabinetry and a plank table large enough to seat ten over by the wide window. It was strangely welcoming.

Heat assaulted her left side. She turned to see a vintage wood cookstove like something out of an antique store. A black kettle burbled on the cast iron top, while several white and chrome doors indicated cubbies in the body. Did people really still live like this?

Denae turned to ask Carmen about it, but her friend was busy separating a mound of dough into two parts at the table, her back to Denae.

Carmen glanced at her daughter. "The dough is ready to spread out into the pizza pans. Juliana, wash your hands, and you can help."

The little girl ran to the sink and climbed onto a stool to reach the faucet. When she was done, Denae squirted a little dish soap in her own hands and washed up, too. "What can I do?"

"You can prep one pizza, and Juliana and I will do the other." Carmen plopped a hunk of dough onto one round pan. "You can use a rolling pin if you want, but I usually just squish it flat with my hands."

Juliana scooted the stool over, climbed up, and smooshed into the dough with both hands, a wide grin on her little face.

If a five-year-old could do it, surely Denae could. Keeping an eye on Juliana, Denae followed suit. The dough felt strange, a bit stretchy, and so pale she knew there was no whole grain flour in it. That would have salved her conscience, if only a little. Soon she'd spread the dough evenly over the pan and added a low rim around the edge like Carmen had done. There. That wasn't so bad.

She nudged the pan further onto the table. "Now what?"

"Don't tell me you've never made homemade pizza before."

Deep breath. "I've never made homemade pizza before."

Carmen paused, her hand halfway to a jar of tomato sauce, and stared hard at Denae. "You're serious."

"We just ordered it in."

"You obviously didn't live thirty miles up a mountain road."

Denae chuckled. "You're right. But Standing Rock is nearly as far out of town, and I remember my stepmom coming home with a box from Izzie's Pizza. She didn't care for the frozen ones." Whereas Mom's freezer was stacked with the things.

"I don't blame her for that." Carmen shook her head, picked up the jar, and scooped sauce first onto Denae's round then onto hers. Juliana smeared it around with the back of a spoon.

Denae nudged hers closer to the little girl. "You're so good at that. Want to do this one, too?"

"Okay." Juliana bit her lip, focusing hard, and carried on.

"Is it weird having someone else living at Standing Rock? Your dad owned that place for a long time, didn't he?"

Mostly because it was Trevor, but she wouldn't tell Carmen that. "Dad and Michelle owned it for almost fifteen years. At first they used it as a weekend getaway before Michelle talked Dad into moving here full-time. But Dad hated being away from the city. In the end, they compromised and bought an acreage just out of Missoula. Michelle still has a place for her horses, and Dad can put in all the hours at the office that his little heart desires."

"And the Delgados bought Standing Rock."

"Yep."

Carmen sprinkled chopped mushrooms over the tomato sauce. "Does it still look the same?"

"I haven't been up there. Not to the house."

"How come?"

Because... why? Maybe because it was sure to have changed. Or maybe it hadn't, and too many memories of all kinds would come rushing back. Denae shifted from one foot to the other. Still, if she wanted to see where things could go with Trevor, that involved Standing Rock, too.

"Sure a big house for one guy alone," Carmen went on.

It had been very spacious for a couple with a teenage daughter. It could only rattle with just Trevor. But what was Carmen really saying? Denae narrowed her gaze and watched Carmen fork caramelized onions onto the pizza. Might as well come right out and ask, so she'd know what she was up against. "Do you have a thing for Trevor?"

Carmen gave her a shocked look. "No way."

"Why not? He seems to be a nice guy, has his own ranch with lots of room for you and Juliana and a pile more kids. What's not to love?"

"Him." Carmen shook her head and glanced toward the doorway to the front room. She lowered her voice. "Besides, I'm entrenched here at the Rocking H. I don't need a man with land and a house. I need someone who'll convince Uncle Howard to bequeath this spread to Juliana and me."

It was Denae's turn to frown. "What do you mean?"

Carmen sighed. "Howard and Madge never had any kids, but two of Howard's brothers each had a son, and they each had one son. Eric grew up here and loved everything about the ranch, while his cousin rarely visited. This was all supposed to go to Eric, but then he was killed..." Carmen closed her eyes.

"I'm sorry." Denae rested her hand on Carmen's arm. "It's none of my business, really."

"It's okay. After Eric's death, Uncle Howard changed his will in favor of Eric's second cousin, Spencer. Which makes sense, kind of, I guess."

"In what universe?"

"In the universe where men rule the world. Where a woman's place is in the kitchen."

"And because you're not his flesh-and-blood? But Juliana is."

"I know, right? But even if I were his great-niece, I'm not sure it would make a difference. He firmly believes that only a strong, able man can be a rancher. He needs to be able to do it all himself, from riding the range to fixing fences to cutting hay to fixing tractors to branding and butchering."

Denae let out a low whistle. "That's a lot for any one person to do."

"Oh, he can employ others, but he has to be able to do any of it. A woman who can cook, garden, clean the house, and raise the kids is a good companion for that man."

"I just can't even..."

"I know. Trust me, I know. I've tried to convince him ranching in the twenty-first century takes a good head for business. Everything else can be hired out. But he's stuck."

"Why are you still here then?"

"Crazy, right? Hoping he'll change his mind when he sees how competent I am? But someone needs to look after him, too. He's definitely not as able as he was three years ago when Juliana and I moved in to take care of him. And I love this place. It was Eric's home much of his life. I'm not giving up without a fight."

"Kudos to you, girlfriend. If there's anything I can do to help, let me know."

"How're you at roping and riding and branding?"

Denae laughed. "No skills there, I'm afraid."

Juliana had dumped all the pepperoni on one of the pizzas, and Carmen began the process of evening out the meat. "Or maybe I'm hoping to convince Eric's cousin that he should defer to me."

Interesting thought. "Is that likely?"

Carmen shrugged. "Probably not, but a girl can hope. Spencer is an accountant in Dallas. What would he do with a ranch? He came for our wedding and to Eric's funeral. Otherwise he hasn't set foot here in who knows how long."

"It does sound crazy."

"Anyway, that's why I'm not interested in Trevor Delgado. I just can't give up on the Rocking H. But that doesn't mean Trevor doesn't need a wife." She cast a side-long glance at Denae as Juliana hopped down and darted from the kitchen.

"Don't get any ideas." Denae held up both hands. "I've been back in Saddle Springs for the better part of a year, and I'm not sure he and I have had a single one-on-one conversation. Whatever he needs or is looking for, he doesn't see it in me."

Carmen's eyebrows rose as she tilted her face toward Denae. "But you see it in him." It wasn't a question.

She hadn't meant to hand out ammunition to be used against herself. "What does it matter? Is the cheese going on next?" She reached for the bowl of mozzarella.

"It matters." Carmen's voice was quiet. "I'm surprised Lauren hasn't tried to set you two up."

"She was too busy throwing every female at James until she admitted she loved him herself. Then she suddenly lost all interest in matchmaking." It was probably just as well. Lauren's methods had been crude and desperate at best.

Carmen laughed. "True. Yes to the mozz. I'll check the temperature in the cookstove and add a bit more wood if I need to."

"You're seriously baking it in that antique?" Denae glanced at the enameled iron monstrosity. "I've never seen one in use before."

"Of course. Why waste it? This old house doesn't have central heat, so we keep a blaze going here and in the wood heater in the front room through the winter. It's so cozy."

"Who cuts the wood?"

Carmen rolled her eyes. "To Uncle Howard's dismay, I ordered a logging truckload of firewood last fall. While I'm happy to wield a splitting axe, I'm not so into trekking around in the forest with a chainsaw and a child."

"You're full of surprises."

"Am I?" Carmen grabbed a potholder then lifted a circle from the stovetop with an iron lifter. She poked several small pieces of wood inside and replaced the circle. "Welcome to my life. Yours seems as strange to me as mine does to you." She grinned at Denae.

Fair enough. Denae arranged a thin, neat layer of shredded cheese on top of the meat and vegetables.

Carmen nudged her aside and dumped a double handful on top. "Load it up — no skimping." She spread it loosely, picked up the pan, and tucked it in the oven.

So much for trying to keep the calorie count down. "Would you like a salad while we wait for it to cook?"

"Sure. Sounds good. What have you got there?" She peered at the bag. "Looks like we need some croutons and cheese on that."

"Oh, not for me, thanks." Denae tore the top off the bag.

"Will you hate me if I'm blunt?"

Denae stared at the salad in her trembling hands. What could she say to that? Because she knew what was coming.

"Are you anorexic? I thought you were naturally thin, but I'm not so sure anymore."

She took a deep breath and let it out long and slow. "It's something I've struggled with, yes."

"I'm sorry." Carmen's voice softened. "Have you found any help?"

"I saw a counselor in Missoula for a while." And a shrink.

"And since you moved?"

Denae shook her head. "Things were better, but I'm not sure... if it's something you ever get completely over."

"I'm sorry, hon." Carmen's arm came around her shoulder with a gentle hug.

"Growing up, I had a friend who was seriously over-weight. The more she ate, the less I did. Kind of like if we averaged out to a healthy weight, the universe would stay in balance."

Carmen spread cheese over the second pizza.

People ate pizza all the time. Not everyone who did was fat. One piece — even two — wasn't likely to make Denae's clothes too tight. Spicy, delectable aromas drifted from the stove, mingling with the wood smoke. It even smelled delicious.

She could do this.

"If you ever need to talk, hon, I'm right here. Admittedly *here* is half an hour from town, but there's always texting and phone calls as well."

"Thanks. Lauren doesn't understand." Neither did Sadie.

"I can't claim I do, either, but I'm willing to learn. And I'm willing to be a friend."

Tears choked Denae's throat, and all she could do was nod.

CHAPTER 5

"U nca Twevuh! Unca Twevuh!" Jericho smashed into Trevor's knees, slamming him back against the door. Thankfully, he'd shut it, or he'd be on his back on the stone steps. The kid packed a wallop.

"Hey, bucko." Trevor grabbed the cowpoke under the arms and swung him in a circle. Good thing his parents' foyer was spacious. "How's my favorite nephew?"

The little guy giggled. "Playing wi' Harmony."

"You sure like having a big sister, don't you?"

"Like sister." Jericho nodded firmly.

Trevor's gaze landed on Harmony, standing in the doorway to the great room, hands twisted in front of her. He held out one hand to the seven-year-old while dangling Jericho against his other hip.

She smiled sweetly and came for a gentle hug. "Did you come to play with us, Uncle Trevor?"

"I sure did. Your dad and mom went out tonight, and your grandma is too old to keep up with you two."

"I heard that, Trevor Russell!" Mom called from the kitchen.

Trevor set Jericho down and squatted between the two kids. "Does Grandma crawl around on the floor, pretending to be a mustang, and let you ride her back?"

Jericho shook his head.

"Does she build stables with every block you have and make enough stalls for all your toy horses?"

Jericho shook his head again, eyes dancing. "Only you, Unca Twevuh!"

Well, and Sawyer, on the rare occasions he deigned to visit Eaglecrest. Trevor shoved the thought out of his mind. Tonight was for forgetting it was Valentine's Day and, as always, there was no significant other in his life. Tonight he'd be glad Kade and Cheri could get away for a few hours, since that would be limited once the baby arrived, and just have fun with the two little people in his life. He might as well be the favorite uncle, since, at this rate, he'd never have his own kids. He was nearly thirty-two. How had that happened?

He parked his cowboy boots off to the side and his hat on Jericho's head. "Lead on, pardner."

"Supper's ready," called Mom. "You kids wash up, okay?"

"Okay, Gamma." Jericho darted around the corner toward the powder room, Harmony on his heels.

Trevor followed more sedately and entered the kitchen. "Smells good." He draped his arm over his mother's shoulders.

"Jericho requested pasghetti and meatballs. Sorry if you were hoping for something fancier."

"The kid has great taste. Plus, I see you've got all the food groups covered. Want me to do the honors of broiling the garlic toast?"

"Sure." She gave the sauce one more stir. "I'll set the salad out."

Dad ambled in from the study. "Ready for me to drain the pasta?" He kissed Mom's cheek as the kids charged back into the room.

"Yes, please." She smiled at him.

Trevor turned away and slid the pan of prepped garlic bread under the broiler. How pathetic was it spending Valentine's Day with his parents? Yeah, he could say it was to help out with the munchkins, but the reality was it beat being home alone... thinking about the woman who'd grown up in that house.

Which was all kinds of silly, since he wasn't going to do anything about it.

Take a risk, Trevor, or quit thinking about her.

He didn't do risks, not anymore, so the choice was clear. Only she refused to get out of his head.

But what if he did take a risk? What if old set-in-his-ways Trevor could find love and be as happy as his little brother? As his parents? Love didn't often come easy. Look at James and Lauren...

"Trevor! Toast is burning."

He yanked the oven door open and pulled out the pan amid a billow of dark smoke. "Not burned... exactly. It's just the way I like it."

"What the black stuff, Unca Twevuh?"

Sure, perfect Kade never burned the toast. "It's not black. It's dark brown."

Mom shook her head. "Scrape the worst of it, please. That was my last loaf of French bread, so it will have to do."

"Sorry," he mumbled, feeling the heat crawl up his neck.

"Now if you were Kade or Sawyer and that happened, I'd be sure you were daydreaming about a woman."

"Not me." Much. Using the dull edge of a table knife, he scraped carbon off the toast into the sink.

She tapped his arm gently on the way by. "Maybe you should be."

"Don't start, Mom."

"I won't. I mention it to the Lord every day. He can manage things far better than I ever could."

"Save it for Sawyer."

She skewered him with a look as Dad gathered the kids to the table. "Can't I pray for all three of my boys? Different men. Different needs. God can handle them all."

"And you think my biggest need is to daydream about a woman?" He tried for a light tone. Likely failed.

"Not quite what I said, son."

He bit his tongue and set the last piece of salvaged toast on the plate beside him. Then he glanced at his mother. "I'm sorry. I do appreciate your prayers."

"Tanku God for food amen," shouted Jericho, bouncing on his booster seat.

Trevor chuckled. "I guess that's our cue." He carried the toast to the table while Mom grabbed the croutons and grated parmesan for the Caesar salad. Dad was already dishing pasta for the kids. Which was right, being thankful for the family he had, or wishing — no, praying — for his own wife and children?

It didn't look like God trusted him with love, not after he'd blown it so badly by panting after someone who was all wrong. Trevor wasn't like Kade, who seemed to always put the needs of others ahead of his own — look at the situation with Daniela for proof his brother deserved sainthood. No wonder God brought Cheri back to Kade and blessed him.

But did God forgive those who asked, or did He not? The Bible was pretty clear on that. *If we confess our sins* — and Trevor had — *He is faithful and just and will forgive us our sins and purify us from all unrighteousness.* Straight out of First John. He'd memorized it in kids' club way back when, along with dozens of other verses. Now all he had to do was hang onto the words.

And forgive himself.

"Have another piece." Carmen nudged the pan across the plank table.

"That's okay. One's enough." It had been super tasty, with the rich roasted tomato sauce and the spicy bits of pepperoni and the caramelized onions and mushrooms and peppers.

"Even Juliana's on her second." Carmen stared straight at Denae. "I have a hard time believing you're full up."

A lifetime of small portions kept Denae's capacity

small. Too bad her abdomen still pooched out no matter what she ate... or didn't.

Carmen waited.

Juliana leaned over her plate, a smear of sauce on her adorable face, a wedge of pizza halfway to her mouth and paused, looking between them.

Howard grunted, his bushy eyebrows forming a gully as he stared at her from unyielding dark eyes.

"Maybe half a piece." She'd regret it later, no doubt. In fact, she regretted it already, even before Carmen carved a slice and slid the larger section onto her plate. Definitely more than half, but Denae knew when to hold 'em and when to fold 'em as the old Kenny Rogers gambling song went.

Yep, it was always a fine line between society's expectations and what she saw in the mirror. But she could exist on chicken broth and water tomorrow to make up for this pizza, right?

Battle raged. She knew better. Knew that wasn't the healthy response. Knew that the numbers on her scale were considered low for a woman her height. Knew she'd swung the pendulum much too far the opposite direction from her friend Sadie. Sadie had found health and balance — oh, and the love of a great guy — while Denae soldiered on.

"Isn't it yummy, Miss Denae? My mommy makes the best pizza ever." Juliana beamed at her mom and took a giant bite.

"Thanks, sweetie." Carmen wrinkled her nose at Juliana in a grin then turned to Howard. "Would you like more?"

He grunted. "Thought you were gonna put salami on one. That other's too spicy."

"I'm sorry. I thought there was another link of salami in the freezer, but we're out. I've already put it on the grocery list for next time."

"Huh." He pushed his plate away.

Finding the pepperoni too spicy hadn't stopped him from eating three slices, though he'd refused the salad beforehand.

Why did Carmen put up with this old man who didn't appreciate a thing she did for him? Was she that desperate for a place to live and raise her child? Try as she might, Denae couldn't remember her friend ever mentioning her life before Eric. She must have a family. Everyone did.

Denae's family was definitely messed up, but maybe she had it pretty good compared to some other people. By all appearances, Dad and Michelle were happy. They'd been together for nearly twenty years and weathered a few storms. Denae cringed with guilt when she thought of her mother staying with Mark all these years, but Mom seemed blind. It wasn't as though she didn't know better. She even had a counseling degree, but that didn't keep her from living in la-la-land. Thankfully, Denae didn't need to be part of their life on a daily basis anymore, nor the lives of her surly teen half-brothers. She had a few cousins on her mom's side whom she rarely saw now that their common bond, Grandma Essery, had passed away.

Dysfunctional came in many varieties.

Right. The pizza stared up at her from her plate, the pepperoni pieces like beady little eyes in a furry head of melted cheese. Denae picked up her fork and carved a small bite off the tip. It really was tasty, just way too much. Way too many calories.

She managed to force half of it down before pushing her plate away with an apologetic grimace. "Thank you so much, but I'm stuffed full."

"Huh," mumbled Howard. "Woulda been better with salami and a bit o' pineapple."

"Why, Uncle Howard, I never knew you liked Hawaiian-style pizza."

"That's not Hawaiian. Don't like ham on my pizza."

"I'll remember that for next time." Carmen patted Howard's shoulder as she took his plate. "Can I get you something else?"

"No. I'll live until breakfast."

How could Carmen's eyes not be rolling right out of their sockets? Temptation swirled in Denae to give the old guy a chunk of her mind, and she wasn't even the one related to him. Not that her friend was either, technically. Wow, Carmen needed a new life far from the Rocking H and the crusty octogenarian who'd measured her worth and found her lacking. How could he not see Carmen's value?

Denae ran hot sudsy water into the sink since there didn't appear to be a dishwasher. Cleaning up would only take a few minutes. Behind her, Howard shuffled from the room, mumbling something about mouthwash, and Denae chomped down on her tongue before she said something nasty in front of Juliana.

"What movie are we watching, Mommy?"

"Miss Denae and I are watching *Stranger Than Fiction*,

and you, my little princess, are getting your jammies on, because it's your bedtime."

"But, Mommy..."

"No buts. Off you go. I'll come read you a story in two minutes."

Denae glanced over her shoulder in time to see Carmen press a finger to Juliana's nose and exchange a sweet smile with her daughter. Denae's mom had yelled at her to get to bed this instant, or else — no stories or songs had ever been uttered — while Michelle had been so indulgent with her young stepdaughter that bedtime hadn't really existed.

There was dysfunctional and then there was dysfunctional.

"Thanks for getting the dishes, Denae. You didn't need to, but thank you. I'll be back in a few. Feel free to start the popcorn if you like while I'm gone."

Denae's hands stilled, buried in the hot, sudsy water. Popcorn? Wasn't she already stuffed with way too much pizza? "You're welcome." If she didn't mention the popcorn, one way or the other, maybe Carmen would forget.

Yeah, little hope of that.

CHAPTER 6

H i, Trevor! What brings you into Missoula?"

Denae. He froze for a second in the process of setting two bags from Good Food Store into his truck. Hopefully she couldn't hear the hammering of his heart. He turned slowly. "Hey there. Had a few errands to run." He thumbed toward the grocery bags and swung the door shut. Maybe she hadn't noticed the black carbon-fiber case on the seat. He could hope. "You?"

She shrugged. "I popped down for the weekend to see Dad and Michelle, but they're both working today." Her eyes sparkled with humor. "So I came shopping. Every girl's dream."

"Oh, yeah? Shopping for what?"

"It doesn't matter, but different from yours, looks like." She leaned closer, peering through the darkened glass of the back window. "What kind of case is that?"

Oh, no. How had she even caught a glimpse of it? "Uh...."

"Ooh, a mystery! I love mysteries. Let me think. It seems like it might be a musical instrument, and that reminds me of talents."

"I believe I disavowed having any talents."

She laughed. "Such a big word for a cowboy."

He narrowed his gaze and crossed his arms. "Being a cowboy doesn't make me dumb or stupid. I've done my share of college." Was still doing it. "Have you?"

At least she turned away from the window, though she leaned against his black truck. Hard to make a polite getaway. Not that he really wanted to, other than that she was snooping, and he didn't trust her.

"I have." She giggled. "I took over half the course-work to become an interior designer then I tossed it all and went for a degree in English. I love being an editor."

"Sounds tedious, always picking at someone else's writing."

"Oh, it's not boring at all. If the story is really good — and many of my clients are bestsellers, so their stories are topnotch — I have to employ tricks of the trade or I'll get so involved I forget I'm supposed to be editing."

"Novels? Now technical writing, I could almost understand."

Denae rolled her eyes. "Not a chance. That would cut my heart out and leave it on a rock for the vultures. But fiction? I can pop over to Paris or Canada or the Texas hill country anytime I want."

His confusion must have shown, because she laughed. "Story worlds. Exotic settings... and ordinary ones that become extraordinary in the hands of talented authors."

"Story worlds?" That's not what came to mind when

he'd heard about her career choice. How could he even contemplate a relationship with a woman who read the kind of junk she did for a living? And yet, here he was, contemplating away.

"Settings for romance and romantic suspense." She didn't look the least bit ashamed, either.

Wasn't all romance suspenseful? Because his palms were clammy just thinking about it. Flight or fight came to mind. Flight would be the best option, despite his attraction to her. *Because* of it. "I, uh, need to get going." He tipped his cowboy hat and took a step back.

"Romance isn't a dirty word, Trevor."

Not sure how she could figure that.

She sighed. "You've known a few people who've fallen in love and gotten married, right? Your brother, for instance. James and Lauren. Others, I'm sure."

"Yeah," he admitted, grudgingly.

"Imagine their story in a romance novel. Just because some characters — or real-life people — hop in and out of bed with half the people they meet doesn't mean that's the definition of romance. I edit novels for Christian authors, and the characters tend to uphold the moral code you and I are familiar with... and what we saw in Kade and Cheri and Lauren and James."

What was she saying? He could feel the heat rise on his cheeks, like he'd spent a July day on horseback cutting calves and sweating up a storm.

"Why, Trevor Delgado. I do believe you're embarrassed to even think about romance." Denae pressed a hand against his chest, branding him even through his denim jacket. "Romance is a beautiful thing, entirely different from sex. Um, I'm sure sex is bea — never mind." She coughed.

He stared at her hand on his chest, long fingers that could dance on a piano's keys or a violin's strings. Fingers that danced instead on a computer keyboard.

"I mean the books I edit don't contain bedroom scenes. They're stories about a woman and a man discovering their attraction and working through the trials that keep them apart, until true love wins all, and they find their happily-ever-afters. They're wholesome stories about an emotional journey, one that often includes learning to trust God with their future."

His gaze took in the flecks of gold on her shapely nails, the silver ring inset with turquoise, the lacy edge of her pink top that disappeared in her navy coat sleeve. Slowly his gaze made its way to her face.

She tilted her head to one side, questions in her dark eyes. The spot on his chest grew cool as she removed her hand and jammed it in her coat pocket. "Trevor? You look like you saw a ghost. That's not the kind of stories I edit, either."

A ghost? Did he? He was staring. He knew it. His heart thumped erratically. Good thing she wasn't touching him anymore, or she'd feel that pulse. Or maybe she had, and that's why she'd withdrawn.

Denae fluttered her fingers in front of his eyes, and he pulled back, focusing. "Um, I'm okay."

"If you're sure." She took a step back, then another.

"I'm sure." But, wait. Hadn't he decided he was done living in seclusion? That he had to step into the light or forever live in shadow? Even God said it wasn't good for a man to be alone. "Do you want to go for lunch? I mean, with me."

She blinked, and her long lashes fluttered against her cheeks. Then a glint of humor flickered into her eyes. "Are you asking me out, Trevor Delgado?"

"For lunch. Since we're both here, in Missoula, and it's almost noon."

"You *are* asking me. I never thought the day would come."

What was that supposed to mean? Trevor opened his mouth to ask then decided he didn't want to know, after all. Because it sounded suspiciously like she'd been aware of him. Aware, and waiting for him to make a move.

DENAE PUSHED a crouton to the side of her salad with a fork. "You haven't told me yet what's in the case in the backseat of your truck."

Across the table from her, Trevor stopped with a forkful of steak halfway to his mouth. "When did you get so nosy?"

"It's called inquisitiveness." She grinned at him. "And I've got an insatiable curiosity. I need to know every-thing." Somehow, she managed to bite off the words *about you* before she uttered them.

"What happened to privacy?" Trevor followed through with the bite, though his dark eyes didn't let go of hers.

"It's good in its place. But is its place between friends?"

He swallowed and took a long drink of his pop, still watching her. "Are we friends?"

What kind of question was that? Denae laid down her fork. "Aren't we?"

Trevor shrugged and sawed off another piece of meat. Guys could sure pack away a mountain of food and not seem to gain an ounce. Running a ranch the size of Eaglecrest and Standing Rock combined would use up a lot of energy, though. More than sitting at a computer, which was why she'd rigged up a standing desk across her treadmill.

She watched him sop up some of the juices with a piece of garlic toast. "Do you have a lot of friends, Trevor? Seems to me you could use another one."

His gaze latched onto hers again. "I like being alone."

"Do you? Really?"

"We're not all like you, Denae."

Duh. Start with male and female and move on from there. What did she and Trevor have in common, really? A love for Standing Rock Ranch, for starters. Was she only intrigued by him because he was a closed book, a mystery she couldn't solve? Or was there something more, something deeper, that drew her to him?

And then the big question was, did he feel the same? Because his signals were so mixed. Every time he seemed to open up a little, he retreated again, just as far and, sometimes, if possible, even further.

"I'm a cowboy, Denae. I spend long hours in the saddle, often alone. I round up cows, fix fences, track predators. A guy like me has to be okay in his own company. I don't need a lot of friends."

Which was all true, no doubt, but she didn't need to buy in. "Is Kade less of a cowboy than you are?"

He pulled back slightly, his gaze narrowing. "No, of course not."

"I'm sure he does all those things, too, and yet he's found time for a family." Oh, man, how had she gone from friends to family?

"Why does everyone compare me to my little brother? My life story is mine, not his."

That, finally, was something personal. Something truly about Trevor. "I'm sorry. I didn't mean it that way."

"Do you have any idea what it was like being followed so closely by a kid who could do no wrong?"

Denae chuckled. "And you were such a rebel?" The very idea was ludicrous.

His eyes darkened.

Wait. What?

Trevor sliced the last of his steak into tiny pieces with intense purpose. "I was never perfect like Kade. He bounced from one thing to another, always caught in scrapes that I extricated him from. And he always landed on his feet."

He was jealous of his little brother. But why? Didn't he know how amazing he was in his own right? "Are you talking about Cheri?"

"Partly." Trevor shrugged but didn't meet her gaze. "The complex situation with Daniela and Cheri and Jericho is part of it. But even before that. Kade has always been like sunshine itself. You just couldn't stay mad at him, even when you tried."

Denae's hand crept across the table and covered

Trevor's. Not that she'd planned to touch him, but the hurting little boy needed comfort, whether he knew it or not. "And by you, you mean *you*, personally."

The curtain fell back over his face. "Tell me about your family. Do you have any siblings?"

So much for that glimpse into the Trevor who hid inside. But maybe there was hope she could get more insight another time. "My parents divorced when I was two."

"I'm sorry."

"It was definitely for the best. They're still barely civil to each other all these years later. Dad was a workaholic. He met Michelle when I was eight or so. She managed what my mom could never do and lured him into slowing down some when they bought Standing Rock. But he couldn't give up his career — being an attorney is who he is at the core — so after trying to juggle his work from the ranch, they eventually moved back to Missoula. They bought an acreage a few miles south of the city so Michelle could keep her horses." Denae shrugged. "They seem content with their life."

"And your mom?"

Drat. She'd been hoping he'd be distracted. "She married Mark round about the same time Dad met Michelle. They had two boys."

"So you know what brothers are like." A hint of humor laced Trevor's voice.

Denae poked at her salad. "Not really. Jordan and Blake are a lot younger than I am. Ten and eleven years respectively. Basically, I was a convenient babysitter."

"No wonder you liked coming to your dad's."

"Until I was old enough for a summer job, yeah. Then I chose Cannon Beach for a time." Memories took her back, some good, others not so much. "I had a best friend there, so that helped."

"The wild Pacific ocean." Trevor grinned as he shook his head. "Hard pick between the Oregon coast and the Montana mountains."

"Not so difficult in the end." She leaned in, her gaze catching on his. "Montana would have won every single time if it weren't for Sadie. We were two lonely kids, misfits who desperately needed a friend." Until the time Mark came with Mom to pick her up from the ranch.

No.

"I can't imagine you the odd one out. You seem so... confident."

Denae angled her head. "Why, thank you. It was hard to come by." And still mostly a projection.

"How?" he asked simply.

"I had a foot in two worlds and never fully belonged in either one. It gives a sense of detachment to a kid."

He nodded. Waited.

She took a deep breath. "It wasn't until I met Jesus that I found where I belonged. It wasn't a place. It wasn't a choice between my dad or my mom. It was a deeper need. Soul deep."

"I get that."

The restaurant and its aromas, noises, and sights faded away. For a long moment, nothing existed besides her and Trevor, staring at each other. No, not staring. Seeing through their eyes and into the true person hiding inside.

What had caused his hurt? Why did he love and admire his brother yet resent him? And what *was* in that black case in the backseat of his truck?

Denae wanted to ask — again — but he'd avoided the question twice now. He didn't want to talk about it. Obviously. Which only piqued her curiosity, the curiosity about Trevor Delgado that grew exponentially every time they came in contact.

She'd find out about that rectangular case sooner or later. For some reason, it seemed linked to knowing who he truly was.

CHAPTER 7

How'd the night shift go?"

Trevor pushed away from the wooden railing in the big Eaglecrest barn and turned to his brother. "Four new calves. All up and sucking."

Kade high-fived him. "Good job. Any of the others looking close now?

"A few are bagged up and in the maternity pen. You'll need to keep an eye on a couple of those heifers. Having never birthed before, they're a bit skittish." He pointed into the far side of the pen before turning toward a nearer cow. "And E44 is pacing and twitching her tail, but she shies away when I come near. Give me a hand moving her to a solo pen?" This one definitely looked uncomfortable with her enlarged udder.

"You've got it. Then you go home and crawl in bed."

Trevor swallowed a yawn. "Sure will." With any luck, he'd even sleep. In the three days since running into Denae down in Missoula, he'd spent far too much time replaying their conversation, seeking deeper meanings.

She'd touched him. Not once, but several times. That hand to his chest. Her hand covering his in sympathy. Or was it empathy? She'd know. She was an editor. He couldn't remember the difference. Her shoulder bumping his as they walked back to her RAV4. Another feathery brush against his arm.

What did it all mean? Nights alone in the calving barn had given little respite from deep thought, and the less he slept, the lower his ability to think through his feelings.

Wait. He had feelings?

"You're dead on your feet, bro. Let's move the cow. Or Dad can help me when he gets up."

Dad had been covering the two-to-ten shift. With the three of them rotating evenly, it made a big difference from the past few years, when Kade had been solely responsible for a baby and then a toddler. Now Jericho was home in bed. He had a loving mother in Cheri and a big sister who cherished him as much as he adored her... freeing Kade to pull his share of the weight around the ranch once again.

Trevor shook his head. "I don't think E44's going to be that long before she calves." He turned from the pen where the youngest herd member, still damp from birth, sucked enthusiastically. "Let's check her."

The larger enclosure was at the end of the alleyway and took up a third of the barn. His gaze snapped right to the cow in question, where a bubble of mucus had formed under her restless tail.

Kade opened an empty stall and kicked a loose bale of hay to cover the floor while Trevor swung a gate across the alley to keep the bovine from bolting past her maternity ward. Then Kade circled around her while Trevor kept the rest of the group away from the opening.

E44 shook her head and pawed at the thick bedding covering the pen, but Kade talked softly to her and got her moving in the right direction. A moment later, Trevor swung both gates shut. He took a moment to watch the other cows, looking for signs other calves were imminent. Satisfied that they had the one who mattered, he turned back.

The cow faced them both, head down. Wary.

"She's not a first-timer, is she?" asked Kade. "I thought we had all the heifers in the other pen."

"We do. She had a bull calf last year." Trevor pointed at the ear tag with the letter showing the cow's birth year. "She's just skittish."

"Duh, I see that now. Well, I'll give her space. You go on home, Trev. I'll call Dad if I need a hand. You're off duty."

"Thanks." Trevor stifled another yawn, but stepping out into the brisk night air pushed his sleepiness away. Dawn was still over an hour away, but yard lights overlooking the corrals and over at his parents' house created pools of visibility.

There'd been a lot of fresh snow overnight, typical for early March at this elevation. He'd driven the Polaris up to Eaglecrest — riding on top of the snow on the snowmobile seemed easier than plowing out the drive for his truck, though he should tackle that this afternoon before returning to the main ranch.

Back at Standing Rock, he fed the horses and opened the stable doors to their outdoor run. They loved playing in the deep snow, but with mountain lion tracks sighted in the area, he didn't dare give them twenty-four hour access, especially when he was away all night.

After entering his empty house, he fixed a mug of chamomile tea with a large dollop of honey. He stared out the breakfast nook's bay window as the darkness slowly faded into daylight, more wide awake than he'd been in the drafty barn.

Didn't that just figure?

His mind drifted to his walk-in closet, and his feet followed along. The shiny new case sat on the shelf above the smaller, scuffed one from his childhood. He'd been too busy to admire his new acquisition. Or maybe he'd been avoiding it.

When was the last time he'd bought himself even a twenty-dollar trinket, let alone spent over two grand on himself? Since never, that's when. At least beyond clothes and boots and household necessities.

He tipped back the lid to reveal the hand-crafted maple violin with its bow. This beauty definitely landed in the once-in-a-lifetime splurge category.

Trevor gulped the rest of his tea and set the mug on a shelf across the closet before reverently lifting the violin from its velvet-lined bed. He'd declined the offer to play it in the store. Said it was a gift, which was true. A birthday gift for himself.

Too many years had passed. He probably didn't remember anything useful, and he hadn't had time to find tutorials online, not with calving season in full swing.

Now, though, he tightened the strings on both violin and bow before tucking the instrument beneath his chin.

He lifted the bow and closed his eyes. *Ode to Joy* felt rusty under his fingers, but he managed to find most of the notes, if not the precise tempo. The second time through was a little stronger.

Joyful, joyful, we adore Thee, God of glory, Lord of love; hearts unfold like flowers before Thee, opening to the sun above. Melt the clouds of sin and sadness; drive the dark of doubt away; giver of immortal gladness, fill us with the light of day!

The lyrics coursed through him as he ran through the piece twice more, but he only recalled snippets of the words from the other verses. He'd look them up later. Memorize them.

He gently set the instrument in its case and stared at it in wonder. Maybe this wasn't a stupid dream, something best buried as he'd tried to do for over twenty years. Wasn't it a sign that the first song that came to mind spoke of joyful adoration to God? He hadn't even thought that picking up a violin again — reopening the door to music — might impact his spiritual life.

It still wasn't a talent.

"HAPPY BIRTHDAY!" Denae hollered along with the rest of the gang then blew into a party horn.

Trevor stopped dead in the doorway of his parents' house, a blush rising unhidden by the stubble on his cheeks.

Man, he looked good. She hadn't seen him for nearly a week, since church the day after running into him in Missoula. He'd ignored her, as per usual.

"Come in, Trevor," his mom said tartly. "We're not heating the entire mountain range, if you please."

He gave his head a shake and pushed the door shut before hanging his hat on the rack above the foyer mirror and yanking off his cowboy boots. When he turned back to the great room, somehow his gaze collided with hers and held for a few seconds before shifting away.

Denae remembered to breathe. She was TSTL, an acronym she'd picked up in the writing and editing world. In fact, she'd scrawled it across a few manuscripts herself when a heroine — or occasionally a hero — trended toward ignorant choices and a serious lack of imagination. *Too stupid to live.* Because wasn't it ironically stereotypical to find herself falling for the strong, silent hero who didn't want her? Who didn't want anyone?

Why would she sabotage herself in the love department? She was far more likely to get somewhere if she turned her charm — though she was beginning to doubt she had any — on Garret Morrison or Bryce Sutherland. Maybe she was too much drama.

She felt a little hand slip into hers and looked down into Juliana's shining eyes. "Miss Denae, Harmony says her grandma is making pizza for Uncle Trevor's birthday!"

"Oh, you'll like that." Denae squatted beside the child. "Is there pepperoni?"

"There is! And all kinds of other stuff. It's all over the counter. Wanna see?"

"All over the counter, sweetie?"

Juliana nodded enthusiastically. "Because then everyone can fix it the way they like it, she said."

Bless Gloria Delgado. There might be a hope of getting out of this party without gaining five pounds. "I'll wait until Mrs. Delgado calls everyone. I don't want to get in her way." Most likely Ruthie, the family's cook, was overseeing everything, anyway.

Juliana pulled Denae's head closer. "And there's *cake*," she breathed in awe. "Chocolate. It's so pretty. Harmony helped decorate it."

"Wow, that's really cool." She felt a whisper of air and glanced up.

Trevor. From her position at Juliana's eye level, he looked way taller than usual. She tried to rise gracefully but failed. His strong hand caught hers and hoisted her to her feet.

"Thanks." She pulled her hand free as Juliana darted away. "Happy birthday."

He offered a rueful grin. "Thanks for coming. My mom never outgrew having birthday parties for her kids. She loves Eaglecrest — don't get me wrong — but I think she'd be just as happy living in the heart of a big city where she could go out with friends every night."

"She seems pretty outgoing. So does Kade, for that matter. I don't really know Sawyer."

He sighed, glancing around the dozen or more people chatting and laughing in small groups. "I'm not so good with crowds."

Denae leaned toward him and gave him a light jab with her elbow. "I'd never have guessed."

Trevor made a show of wincing away. "Yeah, right."

"People aren't so bad. Plus, everyone here is your

friend, right? It's not like she's asking you to make nice with a bunch of weird strangers."

"And you're another one of those social folks."

She grinned at him. "You got it in one." There was no point pretending she was something she wasn't. "And yet, I managed to choose a solitary profession."

"Right. You're an editor."

"All I need is a computer and an internet connection. And friends when my work is done."

"Sounds like the ideal career to me. Other than I hate English, and I'd miss the outdoors too much."

She couldn't help the belly laugh that erupted. "So, perhaps not a match made in heaven, after all."

A shadow flitted across his face, so quickly she nearly missed it. Oh, he didn't want to talk about romance with a single woman who was all but fluttering her eyelashes at him?

Obviously, Trevor needed a little nudge in the right direction. Too bad Lauren had hung up her match-making shingle after her engagement to James. And now that they were married, she barely had a glance to spare for her friends.

Meddling friends. Wasn't that the worst plot device ever for a romance?

Trevor said something, and she was so wrapped up in her thoughts she missed it. Darn. "Pardon me?"

He offered her a lopsided grin. Be still, her heart. "Mom called us for pizza. Come on, pick your toppings, and Dad will get them in the oven."

"Sounds good." She fell into step beside him before realizing that everyone had turned to watch them. To let them go first. Of course. It was Trevor's birthday. He should be first in line. But now everyone would think they were an item.

If she had her way, they would be, so why not go for it? She tucked her hand behind his elbow and leaned closer. "What's your favorite pizza topping?"

Trevor pulled away slightly as he glanced at her in surprise, but not enough to break contact. "Anything meat. Well, to be honest, everything but the kitchen sink."

She quirked a brow. "At the same time?"

He grinned. "Sure, why not?"

Way too much food. Way too many calories even in one slice if it were loaded up like that. But, then again, Trevor had an excellent physique. Tall, broad-shouldered, muscular — she could feel those rippling biceps under her fingers. A guy like him didn't need to worry about weight. He burned off every calorie tossing bales and currying horses.

Must be nice to never need to give it a passing thought.

Trevor guided her into the kitchen where the huge central island was lined with toppings, just as Juliana had said. A stack of personal-size rounds of crust lay at one end beside sheets of parchment paper. Two bowls of pizza sauce came next, then trays of meats and vegetables. Several kinds of shredded cheese sat at the other end, where Trevor's dad stood with a broad spatula and a denim apron emblazoned with *this ain't my first rodeo*.

"The oven's hot," Russ announced. "Load up some pizzas to your liking, and I'll get them on the baking stone. Go ahead, birthday boy." His eyebrows flicked a little as he met Denae's gaze. "And you, Denae. Then everyone else."

She could feel the questions in the air. Every eye seemed to be looking at her, every mind speculating about her and Trevor. Which also meant they were watching her consider the pizza toppings.

First off, the pizza rounds were at least twice too big. From the corner of her eye, she noticed Trevor taking two, placing them on two of the parchment papers, and sliding them to the sauce options.

She couldn't very well cut one in half, could she? There wasn't a knife or rolling cutter. Alrighty, then, she could do this. One round. A dab of sauce, a light sprinkle of cooked chicken breast, a larger mound of veggies, and a skiff of cheese. There was salad on the other side of the island, but she wouldn't likely get away with avoiding the pizza altogether.

Russ's eyebrows rose as he slid her parchment onto the baking stone. "That's it?"

"Yes, sir." And she'd be lucky if she could get half of it down.

CHAPTER 8

No wonder she was so skinny. The girl barely ate enough to keep a bird alive. He'd noticed that before, of course, not only at friendly gatherings but at their impromptu lunch in Missoula. She couldn't possibly think she was overweight. Not when he could probably span her waist with his two hands.

Couldn't he?

The urge to give it a try welled up in him, but he stayed parked in a straight-backed chair with Denae seated beside him.

From the signals she seemed to be sending, she might not mind if he touched her like that, but there was no way he was going to find out, especially in front of all their friends' curious looks. His kid brother had more than an interested gaze. Kade's jaw flicked with a barely suppressed grin and his eyes danced. Questions were coming, and Trevor had no answers.

From habit, Trevor glanced toward Meg, who was

deep in conversation with Kade's wife, Cheri, while their little boys sprawled on the floor at their feet with Jericho's toy horses. Mom made sure to invite everyone even loosely connected to their friends' group. She didn't know about Trevor's history with Meg. All she knew was that Meg was James and Tori's sister and Cheri's friend, so of course she'd invited her, Eli, and the kids.

Trevor's infatuation with Meg had dissipated. She'd changed so much since those days. So had he. Good thing, in both cases. He was older now. Wiser. More mature.

Ready to take a chance again?

His heart shied away from the thought.

Denae glanced at him.

Had he shifted away physically? He looked at her plate, where the remnants of her pizza remained as though blasted by a shotgun at close range. "Not hungry?"

She bit her lip and averted her gaze. "I had a lot of salad."

He'd seen her bowl. In what universe did that classify as *a lot*? Trevor had polished off two pizza rounds and a bowl mounded with salad and was seriously debating going back for more. Knowing Mom and Ruthie, there'd be plenty for seconds and even thirds. He wanted to say something to Denae, but... what? She didn't need probing from him.

Didn't need anything from him.

Did she?

She offered him a tentative smile, unlike her usual breezy self.

Realization dawned. Food was a trigger. She could talk about anything else, but not that. Hmm. "I think Cheri and Lauren have some games planned."

Denae's face lit up. "Oh, I bet that will be fun. They have such good imaginations."

He was right, then. Other topics were safe. "Trust you to like party games. I just hope they don't have anything too embarrassing up their sleeves."

She laughed and poked his arm. "Like you have anything to be shy about. You're good at everything."

His heart swelled a little even as he shook his head in protest. "I hate being the center of attention. That's always Kade's spot. Or Sawyer's."

"How come?"

"Who knows, right? It's just our personalities."

Denae tapped her jaw and raised her eyebrows as she contemplated him.

"Stop it." He shifted. "Don't look at me like you're psychoanalyzing me. You're making me nervous."

She gave him a wide, saucy grin. "I can't help myself."

Because it was him? Or because of the kind of person she was? Wait, now it was him doing the evaluating. "Well, don't," he said lamely.

"Don't what?" Garret asked, pulling up a chair on the other side of Denae and leaning forward.

"Nothing."

Denae laughed. "I'm just trying to figure out what makes the great Trevor Delgado tick, and it's making him uncomfortable."

The *great* Trevor Delgado? Really?

"Horses, I think. Long hours of solitude out on the range." Garret nudged Denae's arm. "Unlike some of us, who prefer people to horses."

A surge of lava boiled up in Trevor. Garret thought *tonight* was good time to make a move? Not on Trevor's watch. Uh... add that to the list to analyze later. He leaned back in his chair and crossed his ankles. "You make your living from horses just as surely as I do, cowpoke."

"Correction. If people didn't need a place to board their horses, Canyon Crossing Stables would be out of business. It's more about humans than equines around our place." He nudged Denae again. "You were talking about buying a horse and needing a place to board it. We've got an opening coming up in May. Want me to hold it for you?"

News to Trevor. "She can bring her horse to Standing Rock if she wants. Lots of room in the stable there."

"You're not really set up for boarding, though." Garret looked from one to the other. "And you're so far out of town."

"Not that much further than you are."

Denae glanced between them.

If he wasn't mistaken, there was a glint of humor in her eyes. Oh, man. He was speaking out of turn.

She turned to Garret. "Do you have any mares for sale?"

Trevor clenched his jaw to keep from replying. Not that Eaglecrest kept any horses that weren't in constant rotation. This time of year, most of the herd resided at the larger Standing Rock stable with its covered riding arena, which offered more space and freedom for the animals with the snow still deep on the mountains. They rotated through working out each mount to keep riders and horses from getting cabin-fevered and bored.

"I can keep an eye out for you," Garret replied. "Any particular breed in mind? Or age?"

"It's been a while since I've ridden regularly, but I enjoy Pippi Longstocking at the Flying Horseshoe."

Garret nodded. "Right. You did well on her on the trail ride last year."

"Are we doing something like that again? That was so fun."

Trevor had turned down the invitation. Sheer stupidity, in retrospect, but back then, Lauren had been set on getting couples paired up by any means possible in her desperation to suppress her growing attraction for James. Why they hadn't just admitted their love to each other instead of all the awkward games was anyone's guess.

Was he doing the same thing?

Trevor glanced sideways at Denae. She gathered her dark hair and tossed it over her shoulder, where it swished well below her shoulder blades. She was pretty. More than skin-deep, too. She was lit from within, had a ready sense of humor, and had an annoying habit of explaining everyone's life as though they were characters in a romance novel.

Annoying? Could it seem endearing if he were on the receiving end?

Crazy thought. Or was it? It had to start somewhere.

Beyond Denae, beyond Garret, his gaze snagged on Eli leaning over to drop a kiss on Meg's lips. Meg grinned up at him. They were good together. God-designed.

Trevor and Meg had never been meant to be. She'd been a rebel, and so had he, just hidden it better. God had kept him safe, even when he'd come so close to tossing overboard everything he believed in for her sake.

Thank You, Lord.

Finally, Trevor really meant it. No more thoughts of what might have been. They'd held him back long enough. Meg was a happily married mother of two and active in ministry at Springs of Living Water Church with other young moms. If she'd wasted any time wishing things had been different with him, she'd been over it for at least five years.

And so was he. Now.

Denae's laughter pulled his gaze back to the side of her face. Trevor wasn't giving Garret Morrison any room for inroads if he could help it.

He slid his arm across the back of her chair and leaned in to join the conversation. "You know who might have a good mare for sale is that breeder over near Polson. Ned Jansen."

Garret looked at him speculatively. "Same place where Tori picked up Coaldust last year?"

"Could be. I'd be glad to give him a call for you if you like, Denae. See what he's got."

She turned toward him, and he pulled back just a smidge. "I'd like that, Trevor. I don't know all the right questions to ask. I had a pinto named Juniper when Dad owned the ranch. She was awesome."

He filed that information away. "We'll see what we can do." He looked Garret straight in the eye. *Whatcha gonna do about that, buddy?*

Garret gave an almost imperceptible nod.

Good. They understood each other.

LAUREN CLAPPED her hands then Tori stuck her fingers in her mouth and gave a shrill whistle.

Denae winced at the piercing sound, but the duo certainly silenced the room. Even little Jericho and Aiden stared, open-mouthed.

"Well, now that we have everyone's attention..." Lauren said into the sudden hush. "It's time for games." She waggled her eyebrows and grinned at Trevor before her gaze slid to Denae.

Uh oh. The matchmaker was on it, now. But maybe Trevor wasn't completely oblivious to Denae, after all. She was pretty sure she wasn't supposed to have caught that exchange a minute ago, but her heart did a little skip at the thought that Garret's random offer had been enough to tip Trevor from undecided to staking his claim.

"We're dividing everyone into two teams." Lauren smirked, just a little, just enough for Denae to catch. "From Garret to Eli, the south side of the room is one team. From Denae to Cheri, the north side of the room is the other team."

And, just like that, Denae and Trevor were on the same team while Garret was on the other. She could kiss Lauren.

"What are we playing?" called Kade.

"Shush and listen." Lauren skewered him with a glare. "We're going to start with Pictionary, but don't worry, we've got lots more planned."

Eli groaned. "I can't even draw a stick figure."

Aiden patted his knee. "I help, Daddy."

Everyone laughed. Trevor shifted in his chair, his knee bumping Denae's before pulling away again. She glanced up at his set jaw before giving him a nudge. "I bet you're good at this," she whispered.

His eyes snapped to hers, deep, dark, and impenetrable.

Whoa. Intense. She could drown in that deep well and never come up for air — a romance cliché she'd never quite believed before.

"I'm not good at anything," he murmured. "Remember? No talents."

She managed to smile. "I find that impossible to believe."

A hint of humor flickered. "You calling me a liar?"

"Perhaps unenlightened."

"Big word."

"I know a few more."

Definitely a glint of a grin now. "I'd like to hear more of your expansive vocabulary."

Denae dared lean just close enough to feel the heat of his arm through her sweater sleeve. "You're on, cowboy. There's more where that came from."

"Oh, yeah?" His chin lifted in challenge. "Wanna share it with me Sunday night? Over dinner?"

She sucked in a sharp breath and nearly choked on it. "You're asking me out. On a date."

"Hello?" Tori called. "If we could get the teams to gather around your whiteboards sometime soon, that would be great."

Denae didn't even want to know if every eye in the room had noticed Trevor and her in deep conversation. It had been too noisy for them to be overheard. But... she didn't really care. There was nothing to be ashamed of. She surged to her feet and marched over to her team, aware of Trevor at her heels. She brushed her hands together. "Let's do this thing."

Tori flipped the dry-erase marker at her. "I hear a volunteer to lead off."

"Sure. Be warned that I'm no artist, but I guess it's cheating to make Cheri draw them all."

Kade chuckled and pulled his rotund wife to his side. "Go for it, Denae. Tori won the toss, so we're up first."

Both teams' markers sat on the first yellow square, designating a person, place, or thing. Denae pulled the first card out of the box, noting the all-play arrow next to *newlywed* on the yellow line. How on earth was she going to draw *that* quickly?

She held the card, print side down, toward the other team. "All play. Who's drawing for your team?"

Meg reached for the card and glanced at it, her eyebrows flickering.

Exactly.

"And go." Lauren flipped the egg timer over.

Denae quickly drew two stick figures and gave one a

squiggly circle near the middle. That was a bouquet, right?

"Wedding," called Tori.

"Bride," said Cheri.

They were in the ballpark, at least. Denae shook her head, circled the couple, then drew a big arrow away from them.

"Newlywed!" shouted Carmen from the other team.

Drat. Denae glanced at Meg's sketch. It was worse than hers. How had Carmen ever guessed?

The other team rolled their die and carried on by guessing *roundup*, *splash*, and *imagination* before losing their turn.

Trevor plucked a card out of the box. His gaze flicked to hers and a flush rose on his cheeks. He grabbed the marker as Lauren called time.

Okay, one stick figure person. Male by the fact he hadn't given it a triangle skirt.

The team called out "man," "guy," "male," but Trevor kept shaking his head.

Those words wouldn't embarrass him, though. What would?

He drew a girl stick figure beside it, but circled the male.

"Groom," said Denae, though the girl didn't look like a bride. Even she'd done a better job.

He shook his head, staring at the whiteboard for a minute. Then he put a single flower in the guy's hand.

"Boyfriend," announced Tori.

"Yup." Trevor handed the marker to Kade and

stepped to the back of the group, not meeting Denae's gaze.

She nudged him, and his gaze flicked off hers. "Not such a hard word, after all."

"That's what you think."

Now, what was she supposed to make of that?

CHAPTER 9

Trevor brought Ebony to a halt beside Kade and leaned over to pat the gelding's neck. "Easy, boy." He swung his leg over the saddle and dismounted.

"He's looking good," observed Kade, pushing his cowboy hat back a little. He ran his hands down Ebony's leg and lifted his hoof. "Can't even tell he was favoring this leg last week."

"No, it seems completely healed. Giving them all plenty of access to the riding arena has helped them stay in shape despite winter dragging on."

"And not so bored."

"That, too." Trevor poked his chin toward Dazzle. "Going to get on her and give her a workout?"

Kade nodded as he straightened but didn't move toward the mare. "You seemed a little cozy with Denae at your birthday party."

That two inches of extra height came in mighty

handy at moments like this. Trevor looked down at his little brother. "And that's a problem how?"

A grin broke out across Kade's face. "And you're not even in denial. What kind of miracle is this?"

"The kind where you keep your mouth shut and don't make a big deal of it?"

"Right." Kade chuckled. "Never saw this one coming. She doesn't really seem your type."

A glimpse of Meg danced through Trevor's mind and disappeared. "I don't think I've dated enough to *have* a type." At least, not one his brother would know about.

"Which is why this is all the more surprising." Kade clouted him on the shoulder, nearly spinning him back against Ebony. "I take it she feels the same?"

Trevor let out a long, loud sigh. "Get on Dazzle already."

"I'm finding this conversation enlightening. The mare can wait her turn."

"There's nothing to tell." Trevor gathered Ebony's reins. "I'm going to brush this boy down while you ride."

Kade stepped in his way. "Not so fast, bro."

"No, seriously. Between you and me and a log stockade? We're going out Sunday night. I'm thinking over to Frontier so there's less chance of being spotted by snoopy gossipers, so don't you be the one to feed the rumor mill."

"Never." The cocky grin slid off Kade's face as he stared in Trevor's eyes. "Be sure you know what you're doing, because she wasn't raised like us. And she sees romance everywhere."

"You think I don't know that? I'm not blind, deaf, or stupid." Trevor took a step closer until his chest bumped his brother's, Ebony breathing over his shoulder. "I also wasn't born yesterday."

"Just—"

"Butt out. Just because you've been married twice doesn't mean you're any smarter than I am. You never dated Denae. You don't know her any more than I do."

Might not be completely true, if Denae had confided in Cheri, and she'd told Kade. But still.

Kade raised both hands in surrender. "Okay, okay. Point taken."

"Good." Trevor shouldered his way past his brother, Ebony clopping at his heels. Whatever that had been about. Behind him, he heard the creak of Dazzle's saddle as Kade mounted up then her hoofbeats as she took off at a trot.

Once in the gelding's roomy box, Trevor slipped Ebony's halter off and reached for the curry comb. The horse shivered in ecstasy as Trevor groomed his sides.

A moment later Trevor realized he was whistling. When was the last time music had snuck up on him? Well, several times since he'd first pulled the violin out of its case the other night. And why not? Denae had snuck up on him, too.

He hadn't been looking for a woman in his life. Not really.

Joyful, joyful, we adore Thee...

He'd looked up the lyrics and committed them to memory so he could think them while he played. He'd be tempted to sing them now if Kade wasn't over in the riding arena where he might overhear.

Was that silly? Did it matter if his brother knew he

was happy and hopeful? Trevor wasn't quite ready to go there. He had a reputation for being surly. Whatever. He knew it and hadn't much cared. What had there been to be optimistic about?

One swish of Denae's long hair, one brush of her shoulder against his arm, one sparkle dancing from her dark eyes, and all his irritability had faded to nothingness. Whoosh. Gone.

DENAE WINCED and held the phone away from her ear as her friend shrieked in excitement. She probably could have heard Sadie all the way from Spokane even without the cell connection.

"He asked you out he asked you out he asked you *out!*"

It seemed safe to bring the phone in closer now that Sadie was babbling instead of squealing. "He did." Denae curled up on the end of her sofa, and Poppy hopped up beside her, resting her head on Denae's thigh. Oh, those velvety spaniel ears. Would Trevor's hair be just as soft? His biceps certainly weren't. She sighed.

"I thought you were going to have to do the asking there for a while."

Denae laughed. "No, that tactic is entirely in your court."

"It wasn't like that!" Sadie sputtered.

"Sure it wasn't. Because you totally asked Peter to that fundraiser banquet as your first date."

"That doesn't count, and you know it. My boss was

pressuring me for a plus-one for that event. Peter wasn't even the first guy I asked."

"It totally *does* count. I mean, that was your first date, and you married the guy. How could it not count?" Had it really been nearly two years ago? Sadie and Peter had had a long engagement and been married for nearly six months already. How time flew, even when Denae wasn't the one being swept off her feet. Maybe her turn had finally come.

"Whatever. We're ancient history." Sadie giggled. "Tell me more about your hunky cowboy."

Denae stared out the window into a gray, rainy afternoon. The view *so* did not match the fireworks in her heart. "I've already told you. Tall, dark, and handsome."

"That could describe thousands of men. It certainly describes Peter."

It was true. Sadie's husband, Peter Santoro, had classic Italian good looks and the charm to match. But as perfect as he was for Denae's best friend, he was no Trevor Delgado.

Trevor.

Denae sighed, closing her eyes, remembering the intensity in his eyes.

"Sounds like I've lost you." Sadie giggled. "Tell me."

"I can't even."

"Try."

What was it about Trevor that made her heart skip a beat? Yeah, he was crazy good-looking, but that was only on the surface. "I don't know where to start."

"Anywhere. They don't have to be in sequential order.

I'm not going over your romance novel with a red pen, Denae."

That made her grin. "Okay. He has a great relationship with his family. His parents like him. Respect him."

"That's huge."

Yeah, it was. Sadie knew as well as Denae did what damage a messed-up family could do. "He works with his dad and his brother every day at the ranch. From things his dad said, Trevor is in charge of some of the operations, and his dad respects his decisions."

"Wow."

"I know. And he and Kade have a good thing going, too. Plus his niece and nephew adore him. He gets right down on the floor and plays with them."

"Sounds like Peter there. His two-year-old nephew, Gavin, thinks he hung the moon."

"Trevor's youngest brother isn't around much. His parents have a whole shelf full of Sawyer's rodeo trophies in the great room and a few framed photos of him in action." Denae might be biased, but she'd seen Trevor on horseback, and she'd be willing to bet he could be as good as his little brother, at least if he put his mind to it.

"Sounds like a story there."

"Probably." Denae hadn't wasted more than two minutes wondering about Sawyer Delgado. Not when his big brother consumed her thoughts every waking minute.

"If Trevor were a hero in one of the romance novels you've edited, how would you classify him?"

Denae giggled. "You know me too well."

"Don't tell me you haven't thought about that."

"He's... maybe a Heathcliff? Only not that brooding."

"Ugh, don't remind me of Mr. Johnson's high school English class. About all I remember about Heathcliff is that he's from *Wuthering Heights* in some dark tragedy set on the English moor."

"That's the one. But he's not quite right, because there's more to Trevor." A whole lot more.

"You said he just turned thirty-two? I wonder why he's still single. Such a great catch, someone should have snapped him up years ago."

"I know, right? But you'd think if he was divorced or widowed someone would have mentioned it by now. Maybe it was unrequited love." Hmm, could that be true? It almost made sense.

"Stranger things have happened."

But who? Someone Denae had met? Lauren would know... but what if it were Lauren herself? What if Trevor had been loving Lauren from afar while Lauren only had eyes for James? After all, Lauren and James's close friendship had been badly strained while each tried to hide their feelings for the other one.

Denae shook her head. Now wasn't that a classic romance trope? A couple afraid to rock their longstanding friendship by declaring love. *Think, Denae. Think.*

That night at The Branding Iron, just after Denae had moved back to Saddle Springs. She and Lauren had gone out for dinner, and Trevor had stopped by at the end of their booth. He'd barely given Denae a glance, he'd been so busy talking to Lauren. About a calf, right? Lauren was a veterinarian, after all. Had there been more?

"All this quiet means you're overthinking things."

Sadie chuckled. "The main thing is, his attention is on you now. And he's a solid Christian guy, right?"

"I think so. We haven't discussed that sort of thing one-on-one, but he goes to church, and the gang talks about their walk with God all the time. You know, what they're reading in the Bible and what they're praying about. I can't remember Trevor exactly participating, but then, he's kind of quiet at the best of times. He doesn't look uncomfortable, just thoughtful."

"Sometimes I'm jealous of your *gang*, as you call them."

"Oh, come on. Since you married Peter, you're part of a huge family. Plus, didn't all his friends welcome you in?"

"Well, yes. But it still takes time, and we're all busy——"

"You told me you were going to limit your hours at the office."

"I'm trying, but you know I'll never be partner if I don't put in the time."

Denae scowled at the device in her hand. "I thought you realized there was more to life than work. Does it matter if you're never partner? That you're just a great family lawyer who puts her heart into seeking the best for the kids she's working with?"

"But I could do more——"

"What does Peter think?"

"He wants me to be happy. To chase my dreams."

"He wants you to work eighty-hour weeks and pour all your energy into other people's lives?"

There was silence for a moment. "We were talking about you."

"Not so fast, girlfriend. I'm only going on a first date. I've got plenty of time to back away if Trevor's not the right guy for me. But you married Peter. You better make sure that man knows he is your top love and top priority — after Jesus, of course. Don't you sabotage your marriage, Sadie, for an air castle that won't bring happiness."

"Your dad's a lawyer. Partner and married, both. Are you telling me he's not happy?"

"I'm saying his passion and workaholic tendencies cost him his marriage to my mother then nearly did the same to Michelle before they found a balance that worked. He's happy now, but it was hard earned. You've got a priceless thing in Peter."

"I know." But Sadie's voice was subdued. "Did you know... did you know that happily-ever-after isn't real?"

"What are you talking about?"

"All those romance novels. They end with a ring on her finger and a ride into the sunset, all their problems solved. It's not like that."

"Of course not...." But Denae's words died away. Had she been guilty of perpetuating that myth? Romance novels were a slice in time, from a dramatic meeting through a firestorm to a declaration of forever love. No one really believed life would have no more problems after they'd tied the knot, did they? Did Sadie? "Oh, girlfriend. Tell me what he's done." Because if Peter was backing out of his vows, Denae would zip right over to Spokane and give him a piece of her mind. No one could hurt Sadie and get away with it. Not on her watch.

"It's not Peter. It's me. What if I can't lose the rest of

the weight? What if I can't get pregnant when we want to? What if I'm a terrible mother? Because I sure didn't have the best example."

Nor had Denae. "Don't borrow trouble, sweetie. And don't hold it all in. Share your worries with Peter. Pray with him for answers. Be strong in the Lord together."

Sadie offered a shaky laugh. "I'm so used to doing everything by myself. You know."

Denae did know. Growing up, theirs had been an unlikely friendship. The fat, awkward girl whose parents withheld love, and the skinny, awkward girl shuffled between her parents. Both had clung to fairy tales to escape, but fantasy wasn't enough. The story wasn't over when the girl got the guy. Happily-ever-after wasn't automatic.

She knew that. But she couldn't help the satisfied sigh at the close of a perfectly wrapped-up tale. The sweet sensation that all was right in the fictional world, and she could close the book, knowing their life of bliss was just begun. Secure in their happy ending.

"So, um, tell me where you and Trevor are going for your first date."

"Just dinner." Denae's gut twisted. "In which he'll notice how little I eat, if he hasn't already, so then we'll probably have to talk about that. Blech."

"In the words of a talented romance editor I know, just talk to him. When he asks, tell him."

Denae let out a grunt. "That advice was for someone who's married to the guy, not for a first date. If I dump all my trauma on Trevor, that's all I'll ever get. One date."

"You're more than your clothing size, as you've been

telling me for years. There are plenty of reasons he'd want to keep seeing you. You're sweet, and funny, and—"

"And have more hang-ups than any man wants to put up with."

"You don't know that."

Oh, yes, she did.

CHAPTER 10

Trevor's head felt naked without his cowboy hat. Why hadn't he taken Denae to The Branding Iron where a guy could be himself? Oh, right, because he hadn't wanted all of Saddle Springs to get wind of this date before he and Denae had even figured out if they actually liked each other.

Fine. He liked her. But he was stinkin' uncomfortable sitting across a white linen tablecloth from her. She wore a dress with enough blocks of intersecting black-and-white stripes in varying widths to make him dizzy. The dress ended at an angle over black boots with impossible heels that set her nearly eye-to-eye with him. How could she even walk in those things? By tucking her hand in the crook of his elbow, where, for a brief moment, all had seemed perfect.

The flickering candlelight caught in her eyes as she smiled at him across the table. A smile totally focused on him.

Trevor resisted the urge to loosen the bolo tie his

sister-in-law had talked him into wearing. The white shirt had been bad enough. Man, he needed air in the worst way.

The waiter set a plate of pear slices artfully arranged with goat cheese and pistachios on the table between them. "Enjoy."

Trevor nudged the plate closer to Denae. "Those look good."

"They do." She slid one onto her plate and snipped off a small corner with the side of her fork. "Delicious."

A moment later, he had to agree. The melded flavors were amazing. "Tell me more about your photography," he said, after polishing off one appetizer. "Those shots you showed us a few weeks ago were amazing."

Denae cast him a shy smile before poking at her fruit again. "Thanks."

"It seemed like you were trying to draw their inner beings out through their eyes. Though that sounds creepy when I say it out loud."

"The eyes are windows to the soul, you know."

"I've heard that before. Makes sense." Her soul must be trying to hide something in that case, since her gaze kept sliding from his.

"It was for a pageant."

"Pardon me?" He couldn't have heard her correctly. What normal girl did pageants? Certainly not anyone from Saddle Springs.

"Miss Snowflake, over in Helena." She flashed a quick glance at him. "I competed just before moving here. I needed to showcase a performing talent and something more in the visual arts."

Trevor could only hope he wasn't gaping. "Did you win?" What an inane question. He regretted it before the words left his mouth.

Her head shook slightly. "First runner-up."

He set his fork down and leaned back in his chair, studying her. "Wow. That's... amazing."

Denae's chin came up. "Probably everything you think about pageantry is wrong. It's not a bunch of dumb airheads in high heels and swimsuits. The women are smart and professional and dedicated to making the world a better place."

"I didn't say anything like that."

"You didn't have to."

He reached across the table and tried to gather her hands in his, but she pulled away. "Denae, I was just surprised, that's all. Tell me more."

She shot him a look then took a sip of ice water. "Well, here's the other barrel, then."

Trevor raised his eyebrows. "Okay?"

"I was representing the National Eating Disorders Association."

Wow, did that ever add up. He nodded cautiously. "Tell me about those photos."

"So many women don't feel they're beautiful just the way they are."

Her voice was so low he barely heard her over the classical music swelling from the hidden speakers. Somehow he had the good sense to bite his tongue and let her continue at her own pace.

"Society is hard on women. So are men, and, in reality, *women* are hard on women, too. There are expectations. We are pressured to juggle high-powered careers and families and make it look easy. We need to be smart and funny and good cooks and... perfect."

That couldn't be right. Women expected themselves to be impeccable? *Men* expected it of them? He opened his mouth in protest.

"Do you have sisters, Trevor?"

He blinked. She knew the answer. "No."

"It's real. I'm not making this up. And so some women do everything they can to make sure they're pretty. To control the parts they can."

Lightbulbs danced. "Like being really, really skin... slender."

She pushed the pear slice around on her plate then glanced up at him and nodded. "Now you know."

Anorexic? Bulimic? Some of those disorders had women barfing up their food, right? Was that Denae? She didn't eat enough... Trevor reached across the table and tipped her chin up. Finally her gaze snagged on his. "You're beautiful."

A little grin softened the lines of her mouth. "Sometimes I believe that."

He laughed, holding the connection. "Just wanted to tell you, in case you didn't know. Really."

"Thanks, Trevor. I read about this Australian photographer who combated her own negative self-image with self-portraits then made it into a business. I... well, I needed help, and my psychiatrist thought this might do the trick. It was worth a try. I know it sounds vain. They weren't of my body at first, just my face. Super close-ups. My eyes."

Her eyes were gorgeous. Deep, sparkling brown surrounded by long lashes, accented lightly with makeup, crowned with narrow eyebrows. He drank in the allure of them.

"Then I did a few sittings for friends. My best friend when we were growing up was obese. Crazy, right? We reacted so differently to the stresses in our lives. Sadie finally found help. She's let go of a lot of the excess weight and even got married last fall. We did a few photo shoots together. I hope... I think they helped her to see her own beauty."

What was it about women and beauty? Did guys have the same issues, needing to be handsome, or hot, or whatever the current term was? He didn't think so. A man needed to be warrior strong, ready to defend the woman he loved. How did a guy defend a woman who needed to see herself as beautiful?

Tricky stuff.

Trevor wasn't sure he could navigate it. He could think of a hundred ways he might say the wrong thing. Yeah, he was tough. A cowboy unafraid of green-broke horses and tantrum-prone bulls. He'd face down a mountain lion just as soon as a house cat. But a woman's tender heart? That was something else entirely.

The waiter whisked away the empty hors d'oeuvres plate, topped off their ice water, and set their entrées down. "Anything else? A glass of fine wine, perhaps?"

Trevor shook his head. "No, thank you. We're good." This wasn't a night for wine. It was a night for crystal-clear thinking and careful words. He eyed the salad decked with strips of chicken breast across the table then at his own steak, baked potato, and Caesar. Careful words indeed. He'd start with asking God's blessing on their meal. Out loud, because that was part of being a defender.

DENAE POKED AT HER SALAD. After that conversation — awkward! — Trevor was sure to notice if she didn't eat most of her meal. The chicken had been marinated in a lovely citrusy sauce that complemented the dressing. She could do this, and maybe manage a few bites of the garlic toast she'd neglected to refuse.

Why wasn't she healed? Why did she still mentally add up every calorie in an effort to determine how soon she'd need to buy bigger clothes if this kept up? It wasn't lack of counseling. It wasn't lack of prayer. She knew all the appropriate information, but food was hard. Really hard, even when it tasted good, and this did.

She glanced at Trevor. Her issues weren't keeping him from enjoying his steak or baked potato slathered in butter, sour cream, chives, and bacon bits. A cowboy must burn through a lot of calories, because Trevor was anything but fat. He wasn't skinny, either. Just strong and sturdy and ready for anything.

He met her gaze. "What, do I have sour cream on my chin?" He dabbed his face with his linen napkin.

Denae laughed. "No. I was just admiring... you."

His eyebrows peaked. "Admiring *me?*"

Yep, she'd really said that out loud. "That you're enjoying your meal. Is it good?"

"It's terrific. Want a taste?" He sliced a sliver of beef and held out his fork.

He'd ordered medium-rare. Rather pink for her liking, but she was in too far now. She opened her lips, and he tucked the bite inside. She chewed and swallowed. "Very tender, and a nice flavor."

He nodded, grinning. "Agreed." He forked in another bite. "I don't know much about eating disorders," he said at last. "I'd like to understand."

Hadn't she explained? Too generically, maybe. "I was shuffled back and forth between my parents. I didn't belong anywhere. It didn't seem anything I did was good enough for either of them."

Trevor's gaze stayed steady.

She tried to grab strength from that. "My mom's pretty heavy, and my stepdad seems to really like that. He's always touching her..." Denae fought the grimace. "It's awkward. I made sure he'd never look at me like that. He... his eyes kind of roved." As had his hands. Once.

"So staying thin was self-defense."

"It sounds silly. I mean, I'm not as pretty as my mom, and I was just a kid. So he probably wouldn't have done anything, anyway." She tried to push his measuring smirk out of her mind.

"Denae."

Why had she said all that? She snatched a glance at Trevor's face. Just compassion, not disgust or horror.

"No child should ever have to worry about whether her stepdad is going to cross those lines or not."

"I know. Mark's... just Mark, I guess. He's always looking around, and he plays a bit rough."

"Does your mom know?"

He played rough with Mom, too. What would it take for Mom to open her eyes and realize how negative her life was? She'd once counseled women, but now she worked as a shift manager at a fast-food restaurant. Was that so she wouldn't have to face reality?

Denae grimaced. "She knows. It's not ideal, but it seems to work for them." More or less.

"Denae? I want you to know something about me."

Her stomach churned, threatening to evict the salad she'd consumed. She braced herself. "Yes?"

"I'm not that kind of man. When I marry, I'll be devoted to my wife for the rest of our days. No roving eyes or hands or even thoughts, because God made men and women for a one-on-one commitment. I'll do my best, every single day, to honor the woman I love."

Tears prickled the backs of Denae's eyes. "Good to know."

"Unfortunately, Mark isn't the only jerk out there. But I'm not so unique, either. There are a lot of honorable men, Men who don't think of women as sex objects or something flashy to have on their arm. Men who know there is far more to a woman than her shape."

There *were* men who looked deeper. Her best friend had found one. Peter had seen past Sadie's obesity and into her heart. Had loved her long before she'd lost over one hundred pounds. Could Denae be as lucky as Sadie? Was Trevor the same kind of guy as Peter, who loved a woman for who she was at the core?

Because it had taken Denae a long time to love that woman, the one she'd captured in the camera lens. To see her as beautiful without a shape attached. Not beautiful for a fat girl, or beautiful for a skinny girl, but just beautiful. The way God saw her.

"Was the pageant a good thing, Denae? Did it help... or hinder?"

She blinked at Trevor. "It helped more than it hindered, I think. Once I'd decided to do it and to make eating disorders my focus, I had to publicly face who I was in front of a group of gorgeous women, both the other contestants and the judges. It was hard. Really, really hard."

Trevor nodded. "We can't heal from stuff if we don't admit to it."

"So I figured out. I had several long talks with one of the women who works with the pageant, Marisa Mackie. She was a model for years. Now she and her husband travel the world making documentaries about the food crisis in developing countries, and especially how it relates to kids. Orphans. She's seen food issues from many different angles."

Why was she telling all this to Trevor? Better to get it all out front so he could back away if he wanted to, before anyone got hurt. Before either of them were invested enough in a relationship for that to happen.

Only problem was, it was already too late. They'd met nearly a year ago, and she'd been losing her heart to him, a little at a time, ever since. Now that they were finally sitting across the table from each other on their first real date, it was far too late. Because her heart was all in.

CHAPTER 11

"M ay I offer you dessert?" The waiter hovered at the end of their table.

With a start, Trevor realized they were surrounded by vacant tables, and the few that weren't were occupied by different diners than he'd last noticed. How long had he and Denae sat here, just talking?

He focused on her bright eyes. Knowing what he did now, she wasn't likely to go for it... unless... "Would you like to split something?"

Her gaze softened slightly, but she still hesitated before nodding. "That sounds nice."

The waiter set the dessert menu on the white tablecloth. "And more coffee?"

Trevor glanced at his watch. They'd need to leave in about half an hour so he could relieve his dad for the calving night shift. "Please."

"And for you, ma'am?"

"Chamomile tea would be perfect, thanks."

Once they'd placed an order for an apple compote,

Trevor spoke again. "Just so you know, I'm expected back in the calving barn by ten o'clock. Dad won't mind if I'm a little late." Not that Trevor made a habit of keeping his father waiting.

Denae looked at her black sports watch. "Is calving nearly over for the year? I can't imagine pulling the night shift all the time."

"It's easier to do it for six weeks straight than to switch back and forth. Dad does the evenings, and Kade picks up the day shifts, which works well for him. He's got a few hours for the family before putting the kids to bed."

Just the thought of his little brother reading bedtime stories, singing lullabies, and kissing tousled, sleepy heads always got to Trevor. Not quite as much tonight.

Trevor reached across the table, gathered Denae's hands in his, and stroked her thumbs with his. Would she want children? Was she healthy enough to become pregnant with the eating disorder still dogging her heels? And was he getting too far ahead of himself even wondering these things?

No. He was thirty-two, with Denae only four years behind. He hadn't invited her to dinner on a whim. Casual dating was for guys ten years younger. Which meant he needed to do some research, thinking long and hard about the impact her issues might have on a marriage and family before he got in too deep.

Except he already was.

Before he kissed her, then. Before he made a verbal commitment.

It wasn't like he couldn't have guessed. Ever since she'd returned to Saddle Springs last year, he'd known she was thin. Known she had a tiny appetite. A man with two brain cells could have figured out there was more to it than met the eye.

"Trevor? You're looking at me funny."

He blinked. Yeah, he'd been kind of looking through her, his mind buzzing with all the implications. "I'm sorry. Just thinking."

Denae tried to tug her hands away, but he didn't let go. "Hey, it's okay. I know I'm rather high maintenance. We can just be friends." She stared at the table between them.

Quick prayer. Deep breath. "I want to be your friend."

Her gaze flicked up then away again. "Okay."

"I... I want to be more, too." So much for research and analytical thought. "I really like you, a lot. And I feel like we have a deep connection that could be... uh... more."

Mouth, meet brain. Remember all that about communicating with each other?

This time her eyes pierced his like bullets finding the bulls-eye. Something resembling hope glinted in their depths.

Since when was anything he said this powerful? How could his words, his feelings, impact another human enough to give or take away hope? Huge responsibility. He couldn't take it lightly. He was going to screw up. Most definitely. And the repercussions weren't going to be good when he did.

Oh, Lord, what have I done? How can I live with this responsibility?

And while it was true that Denae had to make her own decisions, seek help, maintain her health, and all those other great self-care things, having someone around who loved her unconditionally — whoa. Talk about his brain getting ahead. Love? He was so not there.

Yet.

But he could be.

TREVOR'S HANDS kept a tight grip on hers, not that Denae wanted to be free, exactly. And his eyes. He was seeing her, not the facade she'd put up years ago and worked so hard to maintain, but the Denae Jordanna Archibald behind it.

The Denae she'd tried to capture in those self-portraits. The Denae she'd revealed on stage at the Miss Snowflake Pageant in that brutal week of being who she really was. Open. Vulnerable. It had been so, so painful, and she could only be thankful she hadn't been crowned the winner. She'd have had to spend an entire year touring and speaking out on behalf of the National Eating Disorders Association. They were worthy. She knew it in every fiber of her being, but that didn't make it easy.

Nothing was easy.

Definitely not laying her soul bare to the one man who had the power to hold it gently or crush it completely. He said he'd be there. That he wanted a deeper relationship. Was that only because he hadn't yet realized the ugliness beneath her facade? Because she couldn't handle that rejection. She just couldn't.

Oh, she knew she was putting too much power into Trevor Delgado's hands. That God was her comfort, and He'd be there even if — when — Trevor walked away and found an easier woman to love.

She knew it.

But her heart feared. She'd never been enough for anyone. Not for her mother, certainly. Not for her busy dad. Just Sadie, and only because her best friend had enough pain and trauma in her life to rival Denae's.

Trevor was perfect, though. A hardworking, well-adjusted man with two parents who loved each other and their sons. Sure, he was quiet and introverted, but everyone liked him.

How could a man like him settle for a mess like her? How long would it last?

"Denae?"

His gentle voice called her back from the dark place she'd been sinking into. His hands still gripped hers, while the vanilla bean ice cream had melted into rivulets on the apple compote beside them.

She dared meet his gaze and managed a smile. "Sorry. Lost in thought."

His mouth quirked to one side in a grin. "I know the feeling. We've covered a lot of ground tonight. Lots to think about. For both of us."

Was that the first step to a let-down? Because she had no concerns about him or his character. It was only she who was unworthy, not him. It wasn't his flaw if he discovered she was too much to deal with. It was hers.

Really, Denae? No man can be that perfect.

She'd edited enough romance novels to know that, at least in theory. Most delved into both main characters' points of view, so she was privy to the hero's thoughts. Or at least how the female author perceived them.

Denae studied Trevor's face. The dark eyes, steady on hers. The clean-shaven face, revealing his strong jaw. The crisp cut of his short brown hair, which was usually hidden beneath his cowboy hat. Pressed white shirt. Bolo tie with a slider inset with turquoise.

This gorgeous man was focused entirely on her, and that made her want to squirm. But she'd already revealed the worst of her problems — her eating disorder — and he was still here. Maybe he wasn't perfect, but he was pretty darn close.

His hands released hers then brought the spoon filled with apple compote toward her face.

She kept her gaze steady on his as she accepted the bite. Sweet with a zing of cinnamon and ginger, mellowed by the creamy melted ice cream. "Tasty."

He took a bite with the same spoon then offered it to her again.

She managed several bites before shaking her head. It was enough.

Trevor nodded slightly and ate most of the remainder, leaving a little on the bottom, probably for her if she changed her mind. Add *thoughtful* to his other virtues.

He leaned back in his chair, the fingers of one hand still twined with hers on the tabletop, while he lifted his coffee cup with the other. "I noticed your dog at the window. Tell me about him?"

Denae blinked. "Her. She's part springer spaniel and part who-knows-what. Her name is Poppy, and Lauren brought her to me last summer. We think she's about four years old or so."

"Did you have dogs growing up?"

She shook her head. "Not at Mom's, until after I left home. My brothers got to be teens and wanted one. They had a bulldog for a few years but had to give it away since no one wanted to walk it or care for it."

Trevor flinched. "Rough on the dog."

"Yeah. That kind of thing happens far too often. It might have even happened to Poppy. She was tied to the back fence at the veterinary clinic one morning when Lauren arrived at work."

"Someone just dumped her?"

"At least they had the good sense to leave her with a vet instead of out in the mountains."

"I suppose that's an improvement, but still."

"I know, right? She's very sweet and had even been spayed. I'm not sure why anyone would have wanted to be rid of her."

"Family circumstances changed, maybe?"

"Who knows? But she's a great companion. Old enough to be patient while I work, and energetic enough to be eager to go for runs."

"I should've known you'd be a runner."

Denae chomped on her lip to prevent herself from saying the wrong thing. "I like to stay active," she said at last. "Besides, everyone needs fresh air and exercise, especially when it's snowed every day for weeks."

"I can't argue. Horseback riding does that for me.

Gets me out of the house and into God's handiwork. Clean mountain air and all that."

She'd ridden enough to know it definitely counted for exercise as well. "We had a great time on the trail ride last year, up in the mountains behind the Flying Horseshoe." She'd harbored a hope Trevor would join the group, but he hadn't. "You should come this time."

"Maybe. You'll have to keep me in the loop of when and who and all that."

"I will. Do you have a dog? A cat, maybe?" She hadn't driven to Standing Rock since her return to Saddle Springs. It seemed awkward, sorting through all her memories while the place was occupied with the cowboy she dreamed of.

"Two big mutts, Ranger and Mickey. Both boys are of indeterminate lineage." A grin creased his face. "Carmen has tried to convince me to get a Border collie or two. She says they'd be a big help herding the cattle. She's probably right, but I'm generally on horseback. Ebony and I can handle most anything."

"The thing with well-trained dogs is you can sit on the back porch, do a bit of whistling, and let the dogs do all the hard work without you."

He laughed then, a deep chuckle that warmed her heart. "A bit simplistic, but a good point. If only I were lazier, that might be a temptation. She does a good job with training them, for sure."

If he wanted to date Carmen, he would have already, right? Instead, he was here with Denae. And Carmen said she wasn't interested in Trevor. Perhaps Denae should stop overthinking it. "She really does. I hope she can find a way to convince Mr. Haviland to bequeath the ranch to her. She sure loves that place."

Trevor shook his head. "Training sheep dogs isn't really what ranching is all about, though."

Denae narrowed her gaze at him. "No, but they've got most of the ranch leased out. She can manage the property as well as anyone."

"I'm sure she can. I think Howard's hoping Spencer will bring it back to its former glory."

"He's a big city accountant!" Denae huffed. "What does he know about ranching? And who says he'll even move here to take over? I'd think a hands-on woman will do far more for the place than a long-distance man."

"Could be," Trevor said easily. "The old man probably has a few good years in him yet. It'll sort itself out, I'm sure."

Was Trevor sensible... or chauvinistic? He didn't have any sisters, so he might not know how capable a woman could be. His mom didn't seem like any sort of pushover, though.

"Perhaps," she conceded. "I just hate to see Carmen and Juliana turned off the ranch. Carmen might not be Howard's blood relative, but her daughter is. It doesn't seem fair."

"Oh, I doubt anyone will kick them off. It's a big place. Lots of room."

The only kicking Denae wanted to do was Trevor, under the table with her pointy boots. But there was no need. She'd definitely confirmed that Trevor had no romantic interest in Carmen, not that she'd been in doubt. She looked at her watch and pushed back her chair, disengaging from his hand. "We should probably be headed back if you're expected at Eaglecrest by ten o'clock."

He gave her a puzzled look as he nodded. "You're right."

CHAPTER 12

A cow lowed and shuffled in the straw. A calf bleated. The pungent aroma of warm bovines, open hay bales, and excrement filled Trevor's nostrils as he strode down the alleyway toward the large pen at the end. Dad must have every light in the barn on. Sure, a guy needed to keep an eye on things, but the lighting was harsh after the dimness in the cab of Trevor's truck as he drove up from Standing Rock.

He'd dropped Denae off forty minutes ago, wondering if he'd said something wrong, wondering if he should kiss her good night, wishing he knew. Then he'd swung past his house and changed into comfy jeans, a ratty T-shirt, and his favorite flannel shirt under his lined denim jacket before plunking his oldest cowboy hat on his head. The shiny boots, black jeans, crisp white shirt, and the white hat were draped on and around the valet stand in his bedroom, making it look like a different man lived there.

This was him. The cowboy ready to work the night

shift, not the spruced-up guy tiptoeing around landmines, holding his breath to impress a lady.

Dad came around the corner by the last gate. "Trevor. There you are."

"Sorry I'm a few minutes late."

"No problem. Thanks for texting me." Dad yawned, pushing his hat further back on his head.

They'd had to set up another satellite dish to bounce cell service into the barn and adjacent stable, but it had been totally worth it.

Trevor poked his chin to indicate the large pen with the expectant mamas milling about. "How are things?"

"You've got five open pens and eight who look like they might calve tonight. I hate to move some of them out into the other pen yet, though." Dad pointed at a pen halfway back down the alley. "C38's bull calf seems a little weak. Slower to get up and suck than I'd like, but probably okay. Just need to keep an eye on him and make sure. And then we've got a couple of new heifers over here."

Trevor walked the circuit with his father, glancing at the notes on the tablet for birth times and information. They ended the tour leaning on the gate into the main pen, pointing out observations about several of the cows.

Dad glanced over. "How was the big date?"

"How did you know Mom was the right person for you?"

"I knew from the first time I saw her at youth group. A bunch of us were doing a scavenger hunt, and I saw her across the ball field. I asked Bill who she was, and he didn't know, so I hiked over there and introduced myself."

Dad chuckled. "Asked her out on the spot. We went bowling the next weekend."

Trevor shook his head. "You're some kind of brave that I'm not." After all, he'd known Denae for ten months before even allowing himself to wonder about her.

"Your mother made it easy."

A sideways glance revealed Dad's sappy grin. "Nothing about Denae Archibald is easy."

Dad turned his focus on Trevor. "I don't think anything's as simple as it was forty years ago. Society's messed up everyone's expectations. We tried to ground you boys out here on the ranch, but it's a different world."

"Yeah, I think it is." Trevor thought of Sawyer, doing his best to hang onto glory while not taking responsibility. He thought of Kade, how Cheri had jilted him, then Daniela had died leaving him with newborn Jericho, then how Cheri had returned years later with young Harmony at her side. Definitely complicated.

"Want to talk?"

Did he? Maybe. Maybe not. "I'm sure Mom's waiting for you. You've put in a long shift out here in the barn already."

"I'm never too busy for my boys. She'll understand."

Okay, then. "Denae's anorexic."

Dad nodded. "Figured as much."

So that left Trevor the one who'd been blindsided by a great personality only to discover the ugly secret. "She's been getting help. A nutritionist. A psychiatrist." Trevor pulled off his hat and scratched his head. "I guess it's not an easy thing to overcome."

"That's what I hear."

"She said it started as a way to keep her stepfather from noticing her. Guess he likes his women... chubbier."

"Women, plural?"

"Apparently Denae's mom knows he's not faithful to her."

Dad spat into the hay. "I can't abide a man like that. God didn't make women as toys for men who want to play around. His plan is for one man and one woman to forge a deep bond based on love and respect and partnership."

"That's what I want. I just don't know if she's the right one."

"Because of the eating disorder?"

Trevor sucked in a deep breath. "Partly. And, well, I'm thirty-two. The days of dating just for a social evening out are behind me."

"You never really did that, anyway."

"No. You're right. It all seems like such a big risk. What if you put everything on the line, and things go south? Like Cheri jilting Kade, when he thought their life together would be awesome."

Dad looked at him sideways. "She messed up. No getting around that. But God didn't abandon Kade. Didn't let Cheri go, either. If they'd married back then, we wouldn't have young Jericho. Or Cheri's daughter, Harmony, for that matter."

Trevor tried not to think about the fling he'd wanted to have with Meg, if only he hadn't been too chicken at the time. See? Even when he tried to rebel, he second-guessed things. Third-guessed them. And on it went.

"Love is a risk, son. There's no two ways about it. If

you don't go all in, you'll never know what might have been."

"So you're saying I should pursue her."

"What does God say?"

"You're talking in circles."

Dad chuckled. "It's not my intent. Pray about it, as I'm sure you have been. Your mother and I have been, too. We'd love to see you settled with a wife and family. Could use a few more grandkids running around the place, you know."

The image of Denae with a belly the size of Cheri's was almost scary. She was so thin. Could she even carry a baby safely? Why hadn't he thought that far? Because he'd been trying to push back — push out — any thought of risk.

"Not that it's all about your mother and me," Dad went on. "We know that, and we don't even want it to be. We're beyond thankful to God that He's given us a family business that two of our sons are part of, that Eaglecrest means as much to you and Kade as it does to Mom and me. As it did to your grandfather and the generations before him. God's blessed us, for sure."

Trevor nodded. "I can't think of anything I'd rather do."

"Because you don't like change? Or because the ranch is in your blood?"

"Can't it be both?" Trevor pushed out a laugh.

"It can. So long as it's a conscious decision, and not something you've slid into because it was expected of you."

"Not at all. I love the ranch. There's nothing that

feeds my soul like the mountains, the fresh air, a horse between my knees, working up a sweat the way God intended it to be."

"And all-nighters in the barn?"

Trevor grinned, shrugging. "Part of the package. I totally understand why I'm the best man of the three of us to pull this shift. I'm younger than you—" he jabbed his elbow lightly at Dad "—and not as tied down as Kade. I really don't mind."

"Just know that if, next year, you've got a new wife, we can swap out these shifts. They don't have to be your duty for eternity."

"Dad!"

"Just sayin'." Dad grinned as he pushed away from the rail. "But about Denae. We'll keep praying for her, and for you, too. God can heal, you know. And He definitely brings guidance when we ask Him for it."

Trevor nodded, swallowing a lump in his throat. "Thanks, Dad."

His father took a few steps down the alley before turning back. "Oh, I almost forgot. Your mother was sorting out some old boxes in the storage room a few days ago and came across my grandfather's old fiddle. As I recall, you were the only one of the boys who took any interest in things like that. Would you like to have it? If not, we might have it appraised. If I remember correctly, it was a decent make."

"Please." Trevor tried to clear the emotion out of his throat. "I'd like to have it."

"Swing by the house in the morning and have breakfast with us. You can take it home with you."

"Thanks, Dad." When his father met his gaze, Trevor nodded. "For everything."

"MICHELLE! I WASN'T EXPECTING YOU." Denae stood in the doorway of her duplex Monday about noon and stared at her stepmom. As always, Michelle looked great in casual but trendy clothes, hair coiled on her head in a messy bun that had likely taken half an hour to perfect. Likewise the natural makeup.

In contrast, Denae knew she looked like she'd just rolled out of bed... because she had. She'd spent too many night hours replaying every word of their conversation over dinner, every twitch of Trevor's eyebrows, every nuance in his expression.

He hadn't kissed her goodnight.

He hadn't asked for another date.

She'd scared the guy off with her eating disorder. What other conclusion could she come to?

Michelle angled her head and looked at Denae appraisingly. "Let me give you half an hour to get ready and then we'll go out for lunch."

No point in telling her stepmom she had deadlines to meet. Today would be iffy even if she were well-rested, which she wasn't. And yet, Michelle had driven over an hour.

Denae stepped aside to allow Michelle entrance then closed the door behind her. "What brings you here? Not that I'm not happy to see you..."

Michelle squatted and caressed Poppy's head between

her two bejeweled hands. "Your dad worried when you didn't pick up his calls last night."

"He phoned?" Denae frowned. Oh, man, she'd turned her cell off so there'd be no distractions during dinner. "I'm so sorry. I was out last night and I guess I forgot to turn my phone back on when I got home." Or this morning.

Michelle glanced up with a grin. "Girls' night out? I told him you were almost certainly just fine."

"Um, no. I mean, I'm fine, but I wasn't hanging out with my girlfriends."

With a final rub to Poppy's ears, Michelle straightened, curiosity gleaming from her eyes. "A date?"

Denae hesitated. "Yes, but I'm pretty sure it's not destined to go anywhere. We had a nice evening, though."

"Anyone your dad and I might know?"

There was no getting out of this. "Trevor Delgado."

"Oh!" Michelle clasped her hands together as her eyes danced with questions. "Now there's a young man from a fine family. Wait. Didn't I hear he married a long-lost flame?"

Denae shook her head. "No, that was Kade. Trevor's younger brother."

"Oh, right. I remember now. She jilted him a week before their wedding and ran off. And then he married someone else a few years later, but she died in childbirth. Poor boy had his share of trials, so I hope he's doing well. But you! And Trevor! That's unexpected."

A girl really needed more sleep to navigate conversations like this. "Why so unexpected? Although, like I said, I doubt it will become more than a friendship."

"Oh, sweetie, why's that? You're a gorgeous woman. Any man would be lucky to have you."

Michelle knew her too well. Knew that it wasn't likely Trevor's perceived flaws holding them back but her own very real ones.

Denae shrugged. "I'll jump in the shower. Poppy will be happy to keep you company while you wait."

Her stepmom pulled her phone out of her Prada handbag and settled onto the sofa, where Poppy jumped up beside her. "Take your time." She fondled the spaniel's ears. "I've got a few business calls to make."

Right, a busy IT consultant like Michelle would have a lot happening on a Monday. Guilt sluiced over Denae along with the shower's hot water. If only she'd checked messages, she could have saved Dad some worry and Michelle a trip to Saddle Springs.

She made short work of her shower, slid into a tunic and leggings, braided her damp hair into a long plait down her back, and dabbed on a bit of makeup. There. She was as ready as she was going to get.

Denae pressed both hands to the edge of the bathroom sink and peered at herself in the mirror. Then she closed her eyes. "Lord? I'm a mess. Please, please help."

A loud, strident voice came from her living room. Poppy barked. What on earth? That sounded like... Mom. Having her and Michelle in the same room together was never a good idea.

Today was not going to be an editing day.

And she should have gotten more sleep.

CHAPTER 13

Denae burst into her living room to see her mom in baggy jeans and a rumpled gray sweatshirt, hands on her hips, staring at Michelle on the sofa. Mom's graying blond hair looked like it had been yanked into a ponytail two days before then attacked by wild creatures.

Michelle tapped a message into her phone then glanced up, meeting Denae's gaze. "There you are, sweetie. Ready? You look great."

Mom whirled to face Denae. "What is *she* doing here?"

"Hi, Mom." Because wasn't that how civilized people greeted each other, accusation-free? "It seems to be the day for folks to drop in on me. Unannounced. And while Dad and Michelle live only an hour away, you're a long way from the Oregon coast. What brings you so far inland?"

Her mother darted a flashing glare at Michelle. "I don't want to talk about it in front of *her*."

All Denae knew was she hadn't done enough praying lately, or God would have prevented this collision on her turf. Wasn't that how God operated? You did your part then He rewarded you. She'd been far too lax lately. There might be a flaw in that theology, but she couldn't put her finger on it at the moment.

"Michelle dropped by to go for lunch. Would you like to join us?" If only her mother would say no, but it was unlikely.

Her stepmom rose, her svelte figure and stylish clothes a stark contrast to Mom's pudginess and sweats. "Please come, Lisa. I'll even pick up the tab. It's been such a long time since we've visited. I hope Mark and the boys are doing well?"

Mom glanced between them, her eyes narrowed and her lips thinned. "I think I'll get settled in here while I wait for Denae to return. I imagine you're headed back to Missoula shortly?"

Settled in? What was that supposed to mean? Denae's gut sank.

Michelle smiled. "In a couple of hours, anyway. I have a client meeting before Stewy gets home from the office." She slid her phone into her handbag. "Ready, sweetie?"

More than. The best thing right now would be to roll over, fall out of bed, and realize she'd had a nightmare. Too bad she was wide awake, and this was reality. "Um, yes. I'm ready. But, Mom, how long are you here for?"

Mom glowered at Michelle for a few seconds. "I'm not sure, honey. We need to talk."

Oh, boy. Trouble in paradise. "My guest room is

upstairs on the left." Denae swiped her phone off the dining table and flicked it on. Yep, all kinds of messages had arrived unheralded, including one from Trevor earlier this morning. The other visible notifications were from Dad and Michelle. Not her mother.

Figured.

Michelle slipped her micro down jacket on and fluttered her fingers at Mom. "Talk to you later."

Mom ignored her.

Denae wished she could ignore them both, but at least *divide and conquer* was a thing. She slid her feet into short boots, grabbed her jacket and purse, and followed Michelle out toward her Audi.

"Your mother doesn't look well," Michelle observed as she remote-started the car.

"No, she doesn't." Denae settled in the passenger seat and pulled her seatbelt in place. There was no point in reminding her stepmom that walking the few blocks to The Munching Moose was good for them. Michelle would rather drive everywhere... including to the gym, later.

"Don't let her mooch off you, sweetie. She seemed pretty vague about her plans. If you need your dad to move her along, just ask. He'd be glad to help."

Wouldn't he, though? To the best of Denae's knowledge, her parents hadn't spoken to each other since her high school graduation ten years back. "It will be fine. I can handle her." That's why she'd moved seven hundred miles away, because dealing with her mother was so simple, to say nothing of Mark.

"If you're sure." Michelle shot her a glance. "Not that

I really want to talk about her. Not since I found out you've got yourself a boyfriend. Tell me everything."

"Not much to tell. He's one of the group of people I've been hanging out with since I moved back here, and we've started to notice each other, that's all. I'm pretty sure watching me dissect my salad last night was more than he could handle."

"Oh, sweetie. I thought you were getting help." She cut the engine in front of The Munching Moose.

"Well, yes. But it's not like flipping a switch." Wouldn't it be nice if it were? She'd stroll into the café and get something as crazy as a burger and fries like her friends.

"What do you usually order here?" Michelle's eyes drilled Denae's. "Salad, am I right?"

Denae nodded, wishing her stepmom hadn't pegged her so well.

"Will you do me a favor? Try their spinach wrap. Last time I was here, they had a great one with lean meat, pepper jack cheese, and lots of veggies. I promise you it's super healthy. Give it a go?" Michelle reached across the console and pressed Denae's hand. "Eat half and take the rest home for later."

"I can try."

"That's all I ask. Now, let's go inside, snag that corner booth, and you tell me all about Trevor Delgado and why you think he's trying to be rid of you after only one date. Because, even if you dumped a bowl of hot soup in his lap, I'm willing to bet you're overanalyzing him."

Denae managed a grin. "No major catastrophes." But he'd sure shut down when she'd explained Carmen's situation to him, which made him as chauvinistic as Howard Haviland. Didn't it?

"Is a guy supposed to kiss a girl on the first date?"

Kade shoved his cowboy hat back on his head, his gaze startled. "What're you talking about, dude? And why are you asking *me*? I am not the king of first dates."

It had been sixteen hours since Trevor had left Denae on her doorstep without that kiss. He'd second-guessed himself all night long, with every round of the dim maternity barn. He'd triple-guessed himself during the daytime when he should have been sleeping, and now, with Kade at Standing Rock to help exercise the horses, he couldn't stop voicing his rising concern.

Trevor shrugged. "Thought you might be more up on protocol than I am."

"You took her out."

"Yeah." It had been going so well, too. Until it hadn't.

"So you either kissed her and wish you hadn't, or didn't and wish you had. Which is it?"

"Didn't." Trevor blew out a long, frustrated breath. "I called her when I woke up an hour ago, and she didn't pick up."

Kade shook his head. "I never thought you and I would be having a conversation like this, bro."

"You've been married twice." Trevor couldn't resist the dig. "And proposed three times. You might be my baby brother—"

"Nope, don't confuse me with Sawyer."

"—but that puts you up on me by quite a bit. So, is it a do or a don't? How badly did I mess up?"

Kade plucked a straw from a nearby bale and began shredding it. "If she's not talking to you, I'm guessing it's about more than whether you kissed her or not."

Trevor slammed his hand against a timber post. "Great. I don't know why I'm even saddling this particular bronc. I'm a greenhorn in this arena."

"Dude. No man knows what he's doing around a female. You can get advice, sure, but God didn't use the same mold to churn out woman after woman. Every one of them is different. Trust me."

"See? I knew your experience would help."

Kade rolled his eyes. "If by helping you meant not helping, sure, glad to be of assistance. The only thing you can do is take your cue from her, and make sure your relationship is focused on God. Oh, and take it slow."

"Like you did, proposing to Cheri when she'd been back at the ranch for barely a month?"

"We had a history. It wasn't like we just met."

"Yeah, you had history all right." Trevor shook his head. Not that he wanted to rehash his brother's decisions. Kade and Cheri had been married over a year now and seemed to have things worked out. Denae, on the other hand...

"Look, bro. You like Denae. That's great. She seems nice. She might have an issue or two, but don't we all?"

"She's anorexic."

Kade nodded. "Yeah, I know. But she's doing better. She told Cheri she's been getting professional help."

Had everyone known except Trevor? But, if she was

getting help, then it shouldn't be a barrier between them. She'd trusted him enough to let him feed her a few bites of dessert last night. Things had been touchy for a bit before that, but they'd been okay. Until she mentioned the situation at the Rocking H.

"What's going on with Howard Haviland?" he asked Kade.

His brother blinked. "What on earth?"

"The old guy. He have dementia or something like that?"

"Not that I've heard. Nice of you to care, but why?"

"Denae's friends with Carmen, and Carmen thinks the old man should give the ranch to her."

"I agree, but it's Howard's decision." Kade tore another piece of straw in pieces. "The Rocking H has been in their family as long as Eaglecrest has been in ours, but Howard and Madge didn't have any kids. Howard's got that other great nephew..."

"Spencer. He's only set foot on the Rocking H a handful of times that I ever heard of, but he's blood. Blood counts."

Kade nodded. "Juliana's blood, too."

"She's just a little kid."

"Yeah, but she'll grow up. Why should her birthright be taken away because Eric died before he could take over the ranch? Makes me wonder if Howard would think differently if Eric had left a son, instead."

Trevor opened his mouth and closed it again. That made sense. Maybe Carmen wasn't gold-digging for herself but for her daughter. Maybe it shouldn't even be called gold-digging in this case.

"I'm sure curious why that conversation came up in the middle of talking about you and Denae."

"She got all passionate about it at dinner last night, and I, uh, might not have said the right things."

"You fought over *Carmen*?" Kade asked incredulously.

"Not fought, exactly. Maybe disagreed."

"Dude."

Trevor spread his hands. "How was I supposed to know this was a lightning-rod topic? And I didn't even think it was a big deal last night, though she was a bit quieter after that."

"So is it a big deal or not? You're not making any sense."

"I don't know, man. I don't know if it was the talk about anorexia, or about Carmen, or whether it was the not-kiss. Or maybe I totally missed some other cue."

"Or maybe it's not about you."

Trevor shot his brother a frustrated glare. "How could it not be about me? We had a date, and now she won't answer her phone."

"There could be reasons."

"Saddle up Dazzle. Let's ride already."

"In a minute. I've still got a question or two."

Of course, he did. "Yeah?"

"Did you *want* to kiss her?"

Trevor reached for Ebony's tack. "Off limits."

His brother parked his elbow on the saddle, anchoring it to the stand. "I don't think so. It's not like we're twelve."

"What, you want to know so you can pray for me?"

Kade smirked. "Don't sound so surprised. Of course,

I pray for you. I want you to be happy, but it's a whole lot more than that."

"Oh?"

"I want you to live in God's will, know His peace and joy every day—"

"Like you do?" Sarcasm leaked out, just a little.

"Not perfect, bro. You know that, but it's still my goal." Kade leaned closer, the humor gone from his face. "Dream a little, Trev. If Denae's the woman for you, it's okay to imagine a future with her. Don't let fear hold you back. Make it happen."

Trevor huffed. "I'm not afraid."

His little brother's eyebrows hiked. "Looks like it from here. Besides, you came to me for advice, and I'm not going to let the opportunity slide by, trust me."

Trevor crossed his arms over his chest. "Hit me with it then."

"You've got it. One, pray. You really, really don't want to move forward if it's not God's will. Two, if you've got peace, then go for it. Kiss her if the time's right — you'll know — and get to know her, who she really is. It's not about if she can make you happy or meet your needs. You know that, right?"

Best to remain noncommittal. "Hmm?"

"God's given men the responsibility of loving their wives like Christ loves the church. There's nothing selfish in that. There's just a whole lot of sacrificial giving." Kade's eyes drilled Trevor's. "And it's worth it. I don't need to tell you I'm not perfect at this stuff. You've known me since I was born. But loving Cheri like that? It's my highest priority, and it keeps sending me back to Jesus' feet to figure out how to do it."

Trevor wanted to make a crack at his brother's imperfections, but he held back. Kade was right. Not only that, the evidence was there to back up his words. Kade was twice the man Trevor was. Forgiving, loving, generous, joyful.

Kade hipchecked Trevor aside and hoisted the saddle off the rack. "Let's ride."

CHAPTER 14

A quick tap sounded on Denae's office door. She glared at it for one long moment before stepping off the treadmill. "Yes?"

Mom's head poked around the door. "Sorry to bother you. Just wanted to check if it's okay if I put a load of laundry in. I didn't have time to catch up before I left Cannon Beach."

"Sure." It was at the tip of Denae's tongue to tell her mom to make herself at home, but she didn't want to give the impression this could be a long-term solution. Just no. She'd listened to Mom's entire sob story after Michelle dropped her off. Mark had roughed her up and was cheating on her, neither for the first time. She'd lost her job through no fault of her own. The boys disrespected her. She couldn't take it anymore, packed up a few things, and drove clear across Oregon and Idaho to Saddle Springs because surely her one and only daughter would understand and help her get her bearings. Mom made no mention of how long she expected that to take, and Denae feared to ask.

Mom was just the kind of woman the safe house was designed to help. For the first time, Denae saw, clearly, why she'd been drawn to raising funds with this organization. And yet, Denae didn't want to help her mother. She wanted her gone.

Because Mark would be next to show up on her doorstep. He certainly wasn't staying here, not after all that history. She'd send him to the Hats Off Motel... but would he be willing to pay for it? Because Denae wasn't. Aargh.

Over on her desk, her phone buzzed, and she glanced at it. Trevor. Not for the first time, but she couldn't answer with Mom standing in the doorway, shifting from one foot to the other. And she didn't know what to say, anyway. Last night had been awkward, and then she'd been ambushed by Michelle and Mom. She was now behind in her work. She had to finish this edit by tomorrow — the author's release date was quickly approaching — but for that she needed to focus. She'd already glanced over the manuscript and spotted a homonym error. The author had written *interest peeked* when she meant *interest piqued*, and Denae hadn't even noticed on her first read. She'd been too distracted. Now she found herself second guessing the entire edit, but she didn't have time to go through the story another time. She'd be lucky to get through it once before the deadline slammed into her.

"Aren't you going to get that?"

"No, I'm not." Denae blinked at her mother. "I'm

working, and when I work, I don't allow interruptions. Whomever it is can leave a voicemail."

The phone beeped. Yes, Trevor was leaving a message. Again.

Mom took a step back, hand over her heart. "Well, I'm *sorry*."

Denae stifled a sigh. "Mom, I have a job." She waved a hand at the laptop on her standing desk straddling the treadmill. "This is due tomorrow. If I miss this deadline, an author misses hers. She has pre-orders in place, and if she misses her upload deadline, the repercussions for her career could be significant. Not only will she be very unhappy and probably never hire me again, she'll tell her friends, and they won't, either."

"It's just a book." Mom frowned.

"It's not just a book. It's a product in a very competitive business."

Mom's head-shake clearly indicated that she had no concept.

Denae glanced at the clock and winced. "I have a lot left to do, and I need to focus. Find what you need. I won't be down for supper. And, if you want to take Poppy for a walk, she'll be delighted. Her lead is by the front door."

"You aren't having supper?" Mom scowled as she gave Denae a once-over. "You need to eat. And stop with the constant exercising."

She couldn't possibly be too skinny if Mark was coming. "I'll grab something later. If you're hungry, don't wait for me."

Silence for a moment. Disapproving, but silence nonetheless.

Denae slipped her headphones on. They weren't hooked up to anything, but her mother didn't need to know that. Hopefully they sent a strong message to leave her alone.

Guilt stabbed her as she stepped onto the treadmill and heard the door click shut. She'd made her mother angry. Did it even count that she'd arrived uninvited and unannounced? If Denae'd had a heads-up, she could have worked around a short visit. But, after doing too much dreaming about Trevor this past week and then spending much of the night wide awake replaying the evening's events and then being ambushed — well, patience was at an all-time low.

Now, where was she in this manuscript? She scanned for her most recent comment in Track Changes. *Piqued.* She needed more than her own interest piqued at this stage. She needed her focus absolutely riveted.

Good luck with that.

WITH KADE GONE for the day, Trevor paced the first floor of his house. He even opened up the pocket doors to the formal living room so he could make complete circuits. When had he been in that room last? Thanks to Elnora, the furniture gleamed with polish, no cobwebs clung to the corners, and the space smelled faintly of lemon.

Denae.

Why was she avoiding him? Was she really that upset

about his response to Carmen's dilemma? Or was it the lack of kiss? It couldn't be that. Could it? How would he ever know if she didn't talk to him?

Meg had quit picking up his calls, too. They'd kept their relationship a secret so, at first when she'd ignored him, he only thought he'd called or texted at a time when she was with someone else.

That had almost certainly been true, since she turned out to be pregnant not long after. He'd been played a fool. While he'd been vacillating, she'd only been flirting. Although, if he'd stepped into her trap, he might be the father of her son. He'd have married her out of honor.

Would it have been honor? Or a sense of pride that he'd been the one to win the mighty Meg, wielder of feminine charms? It wouldn't have been pride when he faced his parents or the church. At the moment, he hadn't much cared, but he also hadn't *quite* been ready to thumb his nose at everything he'd been taught.

Meg and Denae were nothing alike. Denae didn't flirt. Meg had been obsessed with getting guys into her bed. Denae was all about romance, not sex. Maybe she took the romance thing too far, but it was her world, and he had to accept that.

So how did a man go about romancing a woman? He smacked the grand staircase's newel post on the way by. Certainly not by disparaging her friend's problems on their first date. On the eighteenth replay of the conversation, he'd begun to hear it from Denae's side. He should have listened a whole lot more before he'd voiced an opinion.

He'd blown it.

But it couldn't possibly be forever. One strike and he was out, just like that? On an interest that had been building for the better part of a year? No. He couldn't believe it.

Down the hall, around the corner, through the breakfast room, the family room, the living room. Past the staircase. Into the hall. Mickey gave up following him and plopped on the sisal mat by the front door, nose between his paws.

What now? How did a guy apologize for being an insensitive jerk? Flowers. But Florabelle wasn't open in the evening, and nothing but crocuses poked through areas of the yard where the snow had finally melted.

Okay, so not flowers. Not tonight. Ditto chocolates, but Denae probably wouldn't eat them, anyway. He needed some serious lessons in romance.

Or did he? Was he deluding himself by thinking he could become a hero in her eyes? All his romantic dreams had died with Meg's pregnancy, when he'd seen what he'd almost thrown aside... and for what? A chance to be with a woman he knew even then wasn't loyal?

Yeah, he highly doubted she still slept around. She'd rediscovered her childhood faith, mended her relationship with her family, and married Eli. She'd become a model mother, wife, and Christian.

Why was he even thinking about Meg? That had been over for nearly six years, and he hadn't lamented her for long. But tonight, Meg and Denae alternated parading through his thoughts just as he marched in circles through his house.

"Lord?" he said aloud, walking past the front door once again.

The dogs perked up their ears, obviously hopeful he'd stop and pet them or let them out for a run. *Later, boys.*

"I was never the guy who oozed self-confidence. You know that. Half the time when I've lost an opportunity, it's been because I was frozen in indecision. And that's turned out to be a good thing just often enough — like with Meg — that the trait has been validated."

Unlike Kade, who allowed his heart to lead him. Yes, it had led him through some painful times. When Cheri had jilted him way back when. When Daniela had passed away, leaving him with a newborn. But his little brother *felt*, and was now married to the love of his life. The baby that would blend their little family would be born in just a few weeks. The risks seemed worth it.

And then Sawyer, who flitted from one infatuation to another — if the media were to be believed — like Meg had once done. Who swaggered large and loud, whether riding a bull, or partying, or anything else.

Meanwhile, Trevor blocked both risk and emotion from his life. The thought of leaping into the abyss scared him more than a green-broke stallion, an angry bull, or a prowling mountain lion.

"Lord?" he tried again. "Am I smart or foolish?" He felt foolish. He felt like a spectator in his own life. He was thirty-two years old.

Jesus gave everything while knowing humanity would mock Him, scorn Him, even crucify Him. If that wasn't love in action, Trevor didn't know what was. It was so far beyond risk it was laughable. It wasn't like

God didn't know the plan was doomed to all but absolute failure. He could have written off the entire race rather than make a huge sacrifice that so few would respond to.

Yet a spark of hope flickered for those who turned to Jesus in repentance and belief. The spark had been enough for Jesus to enter the planet's history. To come to earth as a helpless infant to grow up and to die for the sins of the people.

Trevor remembered Jericho as a squalling, red-faced, motherless newborn. He remembered Kade in a strange twilight world of grief and love and hope.

His brother was a hero. A self-sacrificing, unassuming, cowboy of a hero, an all-around annoyingly nice guy, and one of Trevor's favorite people. Why couldn't he, Trevor, step up and be half the man his brother was? He wasn't even facing the mind-bending, soul-crushing obstacles Kade had, but how could a guy shine out like gold refined in the fire if no flame existed?

Ranger whined as Trevor completed another circuit. Even the dogs had had enough of his over-thinking everything. He'd circled the house probably twenty times or more and, surprisingly, was back where he'd started, mentally and physically.

He opened the door, and the dogs bounded outside. Mickey turned as if to see if his person was coming, but Trevor closed the door.

This time he strode into the master bedroom closet, lifted the violin case off the shelf, and carried it into the family room where he poked a couple of more split logs into the fireplace. Then he unlatched the case, adjusted the strings and lifted the gorgeous instrument to his shoulder. He drew the bow across it.

Joyful, joyful, we adore You, God of glory, Lord of love; hearts unfold like flowers before You, opening to the sun above.

The lyrics bounded through his mind as the jubilant music flowed from his fingers.

Melt the clouds of sin and sadness; drive the dark of doubt away; giver of immortal gladness, fill us with the light of day!

"Please, Lord," whispered Trevor. "Fill me with Your light. It's not all about me, but about what pleases You."

Always giving and forgiving, ever blessing, ever blest, well-spring of the joy of living, ocean-depth of happy rest!

Giving and forgiving... Trevor needed to see Denae. Talk to her. Find out what he'd done wrong, apologize, beg for that forgiveness.

Loving Father, Christ our Brother, let Your light upon us shine; teach us how to love each other, lift us to the joy divine.

Yeah, that 'love each other' bit wasn't talking about *eros*, romantic love, but about *philia*, brotherly love, and even *agape*, God's love. But without *agape* and *philia*, how long would *eros* last? He arched his bow and ratcheted up a key.

Mortals, join the mighty chorus, which the morning stars began; God's own love is reigning o'er us, joining people hand in hand. Ever singing, march we onward, victors in the midst of strife; joyful music leads us sunward in the triumph song of life.

He could imagine a piano accompaniment supporting the violin's sweet strains. Garret would do it.

Squawk.

The bow groaned unmelodically.

Trevor stared into the dancing flames. Why on earth

was he thinking about music in terms of sharing with others? He was a closet music-lover. In fact, tonight was the first time he'd literally played outside his closet since he'd been a kid.

But... what if? What if he told Denae he'd play in her fundraiser? Would that pave the way to her forgiveness of him?

His gut clenched at the thought of performing in public, with everyone staring at him. But, as he pondered the sensation, he realized it was more excitement than panic.

It was time he stepped up and lived life. In more ways than one.

CHAPTER 15

At five in the morning, Denae powered down her computer, turned off the office light, and stumbled down the stairs. The salad she'd consumed at dusk had long since worn off — Mom had eaten the other half of the spinach wrap — so she pulled a low-calorie protein bar out of the cupboard and escorted Poppy outside.

Brr. She tugged her light jacket close against the mid-April night as she stripped open the little package. This would quiet her tummy and let her sleep for a few hours. Then she'd do a quick review of the edited manuscript and get it sent before noon, which would free her up for the art council meeting at two.

If only she had more entries in the talent show part of the fundraiser. Noela Bergstrom was handling the silent auction. At last count, it sounded like items were flooding in. Not so with the talent show. Apparently it was easier to get people to donate knitted socks than to perform in front of an audience. No wonder the council had been delighted at her offer to head up that section of the fundraiser evening, only six weeks away now.

Denae had a couple of days before she absolutely needed to start her next editing job. She'd spend those days pounding the pavement asking everyone she met to participate. Maybe Pastor Roland would be able to point her to some prospective performers from the church. He was on the planning committee, after all.

Oh. And drag her mother around town with her? Denae couldn't very well ignore her indefinitely. They needed to have that talk Denae had been avoiding since yesterday morning. What would Mom think about her trying to raise funds for a women's shelter? Maybe Mom thought Denae's place was that kind of safe. It wasn't, because Mark knew where she lived.

And Trevor. She'd finally left her phone in her bedroom downstairs so she wouldn't be distracted by his calls and texts. What was she going to do about him? It wasn't just that he hadn't immediately seen things her way with regards to Carmen's plight. It was partly that the old man had rubbed Denae the wrong way the few times she'd been to the Rocking H. Howard thought women couldn't handle anything but housework. Mark thought women were for lording over. And Trevor... hadn't been quick enough to affirm femininity's strength.

He hadn't even tried to kiss her, so she couldn't rebuff him.

But it hadn't even gone that far. He'd escorted her to the door, said good night, turned, and hiked back to his shiny black truck with a typical cowboy swagger, which she couldn't hold against him. She hadn't exactly been warm and welcoming herself.

Denae shivered as Poppy ambled around the yard in the light of the streetlamp as though she had no business to accomplish.

So, Trevor wasn't quite like any of the alpha heroes in the hundreds of romance novels she'd edited or the thousands she'd read. He was an individual, more the boy-next-door type, but he didn't fit that exactly, either.

What made the man tick?

Poppy trotted back to the door, and Denae ushered her inside then checked her water dish. She brushed her teeth and tumbled into bed.

She awoke with a start to knocking on her bedroom door. Seriously? Denae squinted at the clock and sat up with a lurch. Whoa. She hadn't meant to sleep until nine-thirty. "I'm awake," she called out, her voice raspy.

"...flowers!" came Mom's voice.

What? Denae rubbed her eyes. Four hours was not enough sleep, no matter how she sliced it. But flowers? What on earth was Mom talking about? She stumbled to the door, aware her hair had half come undone from yesterday's braid and that she'd slept in her clothes. Yoga pants and a sweatshirt, but still. She needed a shower in the worst way, but it would have to wait until the manuscript was turned in.

Coffee. She needed coffee.

Mom beamed at her from the hallway. "Come see."

Denae followed her to the kitchen where a huge bouquet dwarfed the tiny table. Purple and pink gerbera daisies, white narcissus, and yellow daffodils, set off with luscious greenery, brightened the space. "Wow."

"Aren't they beautiful?" Mom cooed. "You must have a very special young man you haven't told me about."

Denae tugged the card out of the bouquet. *Have a great day! Trevor*

Not exactly an admission of undying love, but she'd take what she could get. And she still hadn't listened to all his messages. Another glance at the clock reminded her that he'd be asleep now after night shift in the calving barn.

The longer she put off talking to him, the more awkward it would be, and it was already notching up there. The least she could do was send a thank-you text and hope he had his phone turned off so the ding wouldn't waken him.

Mom leaned over her shoulder to read the card. "Who's Trevor? Someone special, sounds like."

Denae moved over to the sink and dumped yesterday's coffee grounds into it. "We went out the other night. Seems like a nice guy, but I don't know him that well."

"Looks like a keeper."

"Maybe. We'll see." She finished setting up the coffee pot and flipped it on. "So, today. I'm locking myself back into the office until noon. I've got an art council meeting at two. Want to come?"

Mom stared at her. "Art council? You're not an artist."

Here it came. "The art council is putting on a two-pronged fundraiser in a few weeks. One part is a talent show, and the other is a silent auction. I'm offering a photography package through the silent auction."

Mom's brow furrowed. "So why do you need to go to the meeting?"

"Because I volunteered to coordinate the talent show."

"You?"

"Yes, Mom. Me. I'm good at organizing things, and this is a way I can help."

"Well. That's interesting."

Not half as interesting as the cause behind it, but if Mom didn't ask, Denae wasn't going there. She tried to make her eyes sparkle, but they probably only glittered. "I'm a grownup. I'm an amazing person with talents and experience and everything. The meeting will probably take about two hours so, if you choose not to come, I'll be home in time for supper. This evening you can explain to me just what is going on with you and Mark, and why you're here. And if we should expect him to show up on the doorstep any minute."

Mom looked at the flowers and made a show of sniffing the fragrant blooms.

Bingo.

TREVOR KNOCKED on the office door a second time, shifting from one booted foot to the other as he glanced around Canyon Crossing Stables. The ranch was tidy and neat with classic white board fences crisscrossing the rolling bench-land above the creek. Garret's family offered a great service here, boarding horses for landless horse lovers in Saddle Springs as well as catering to visiting tourists. Where the Carmichaels' ranch, the Flying Horseshoe, was a full resort with cabins around a small lake, offering fishing, swimming, and canoeing as well as riding, Canyon Crossing wasn't a destination.

The door swung open, bringing his attention back to the task at hand. Garret stepped out onto the stoop in the late afternoon sunshine. "Trevor! What brings you here?"

Give the guy credit. There'd never been a moment of awkwardness since Trevor had staked his claim on Denae at his birthday party. Would Garret be quick to move in if things didn't work out? Trevor shoved the thought aside. "I wanted to talk about the art council fundraiser."

Garret blinked. "Uh, sure. What about it?"

"You're performing, right?"

"Yeah. James and I are doing instrumentals to open and close, and I'm accompanying Kade's solo." Garret gave Trevor a long look. "If you're wanting to sing with your brother, maybe it's him you need to talk to."

Trevor shook his head. "It's not that. It's..."

Garret's eyebrows rose, but his expression was mostly curious.

"This is hard. I'd ask you to keep it a secret, but that kind of defeats the purpose of a talent show, right?"

"I'm not following."

"When I was a kid, I had a little half-size violin. I loved that thing. Mom hauled me down into Saddle Springs every week for a lesson. I was pretty good... for a seven-year-old."

"Neat. I didn't know that."

"Sawyer jumped off the top bunk and broke the bow.

I told my mom I was over playing it anyway. It was baby stuff."

Garret's eyebrows rose.

Trevor huffed out a breath. "I was a stupid, insecure kid and gave up the one thing that made me different from my brothers."

"I think there's a story there."

"I'm sure. Anyway, I, uh, bought myself a violin a couple of months ago. Been poking around YouTube picking up tips. Practicing."

Garret's eyes sharpened in interest. "Are you any good?"

"For someone who shut music out of his life for almost twenty-five years and only recently picked it back up?" Man, it was hard blowing his own horn. "I think so, but why don't you be the judge?"

"You brought it?" Garret swung toward Trevor's truck.

"I did. I want to play *Ode to Joy*, and I'd like you to accompany me. At least if it wouldn't embarrass you too badly."

"I doubt that." He jutted his chin toward the truck. "I want to hear."

This was why Trevor had come, but his hands grew clammy as he strode over and pulled open the backdoor. He unsnapped the case, lifted the instrument out of its velvet cradle, and plucked out the bow. His hands shaking, he tightened the strings before turning back to Garret and tucking the violin under his chin.

Garret's low whistle seemed to indicate approval and made Trevor grin, but he couldn't keep talking. It was time to do. He drew the bow across the strings once then closed his eyes and launched into the music. *Joyful, joyful, we adore Thee...*

When the final strains had dissipated in the spring air, he lowered the instrument and turned to Garret.

His friend stood with his hands jammed into his jeans pockets, head tipped to one side. "How long did you say you've been practicing?"

"Uh... six weeks? Maybe two months."

"You're good. You'd be in some famous orchestra by now if you hadn't given it up."

"Oh, I doubt that. It's in my blood, though. My dad's grandfather fiddled for dances all through this area when he was a young buck."

"Amazing." Garret shook his head with an amused grin. "Bring that thing inside and let's see what you sound like with a piano behind you."

"Right now?"

"Why not? You're here; I'm here. Let's give it a whirl."

Garret actually thought he was good? That this wasn't just a reversion to a childish dream? Maybe he'd hoped it would be. That Garret would tell him to go home and enjoy his relaxing little hobby behind closed drapes? Then he wouldn't have to perform. In front of people.

Trevor followed Garret through the foyer and into a room where a baby grand held center stage and shelves held instruments and music. Even the artwork revolved around music.

Garret slid onto the bench and ran through a couple of scales. Then he beckoned Trevor over with a nod of his head. Of course, he hadn't had to ask which key Trevor had played in. Music was part of Garret's core. It had been something Trevor's soul had yearned toward. That he'd denied.

He lifted the violin again, watching Garret's hands, feeling the music. He nodded at Garret when he was ready to jump in, and Garret gentled the piano, allowing the violin to swell above it.

All Your works with joy surround You, earth and heaven reflect Your rays, stars and angels sing around You, center of unbroken praise...

The praise and worship and joy flowed through Trevor's hands. Humans were made to worship God, and music was a beautiful way to express that, like opening the floodway on a dam.

He paused after the third verse while Garret's fingers flew over the keys in a bridge that ended a notch higher. At Garret's nod, Trevor's violin soared into the finale.

They stared at each other in the silence as the last wisp of a note floated away then Garret leaped from the bench, nearly upsetting it, and punched Trevor's shoulder. "That was awesome! Can we do it again?"

"Are you serious? I fumbled the transition between the second and third verses, and squeaked a bit on the fourth." Though, over all, it *had* sounded pretty good.

"That's why we'll practice some more. But, yeah, you don't get a pass, buddy. If you don't get this on Denae's set list for the show, I will. You came to me, and I'm not letting you out of it." Garret dropped back to the bench. "Ready?" He played the first measure then stopped. "What else do you know?"

"Nothing this well. Trust me. One song is enough."

"But—"

"Don't push it, dude." Trevor raised his eyebrows and pointed the bow at his friend.

Garret sighed. "Okay. Fine. You do the intro this time, and I'll work around you. Let's polish this baby."

CHAPTER 16

A woman could starve on this." Mom surveyed the grilled tilapia and the salad of mixed greens. "How late is your grocery store open? If this is supper, I'm going to need to supplement it."

"Eight o'clock." Denae bit the words off. "And you didn't exactly give me any warning that you were coming, so I shopped as I usually do."

"All you have is rabbit food."

"Pretty sure rabbits don't eat fish." Denae set two glasses of ice water on the table. "It's ready."

Mom squeezed lemon slices into her glass. No point in telling her the mountain water was as clean and pure as any on the planet. Or that the lemon had been intended for the fish.

Denae took her seat and bowed her head. "Thank You, Lord, for all Your goodness to us and for providing this food. Please bless Mom and me as we talk. In Jesus' name, amen."

Her mother rolled her eyes. "Bless us? What is that supposed to mean?"

It was going to mean that God would, hopefully, keep Denae from losing her temper and saying things she'd regret. "Tell me what happened back home."

"I told you. I left Mark. I'm done with him chasing anything in a skirt then pushing me around when he gets home. He can't have me and everyone else."

It was about time. The man had never treated Mom right, never been faithful. How could Mom have ever thought him an improvement over Dad?

Denae flaked off a small portion of fish. "Does he know where you are?"

"Why would I tell him that?"

"So, what are your plans?"

"I'm not sure what you mean."

Seriously? "You can stay with me a few more days, if you need to, but that's all. Sadie and Peter are coming to visit soon, and I'll need the guest bedroom back."

"I'm your mother."

"Yes, and I've been an adult for ten years. This is my home, and I'm not looking for a roommate."

"I can't believe it's come to this." Mom dabbed her napkin at her eyes. "When my own daughter doesn't want me around."

"You're welcome to stay in Saddle Springs. Find your own place to rent, find a job." Someplace safely out of Denae's sphere.

"I can't afford a rental."

Denae set her fork down, the little appetite she'd had

long fled. "You inherited quite a chunk from Grandma Essery's estate, plus your share of her house in Spokane."

"Mark..."

Oh, no. "Mark what?"

Mom sniffed. "He gambled it away."

"So you're broke."

Mom nodded. "I used my credit card to come to Montana, but when I went to use it this morning, it didn't go through."

Not only broke, but completely cut off. Great. The only thing that could make this better was Mark showing up on the doorstep... which he was likely to do. He might not be a genius, but it wouldn't take one to figure out where his wife had gone. Where else but to her only daughter? And the trail of credit card receipts would corroborate that.

He wouldn't chase Mom because he loved her. Any thoughts of that had been squashed years ago. He'd follow her because he couldn't stand not to be in control. Because it was fine if he spurned her, but absolutely not okay if she were the one wielding rejection.

Mark was coming. It was only a matter of time, really.

Denae's hands shook. "I'm sorry, Mom. You can't stay here. It's not safe." It felt like her boundaries were crumbling, undoing all the work of the past few years. She couldn't, just couldn't, go through all this again.

"But I have no place else."

"I'll call Pastor Roland and see if he has any suggestions." If only the safe house had already been set up, but it wasn't. Mom definitely fit the parameters. How ironic that she had once counseled women in this exact situation.

"No offense, but I don't want to get involved in any religious thing."

Denae pinned her mother with a look. "You came to me looking for help. That's the only offer I have. That or a full tank of gas and a couple of hundred dollars in cash to see you on the highway out of Saddle Springs."

"I'll consider it." Mom had a bite of salad. "You said Sadie is coming to visit? I haven't seen her in a long time. I guess she won't be back to Cannon Beach now since her father moved out to Spokane to be near his only child."

"Yes, Sadie and her husband are coming."

"I can't believe she managed to snare a man, as heavy as she is."

Denae sighed. "Mom, you *know* that a woman's worth isn't measured by a number on the scale." If she only believed it herself for more than five minutes at a time. "Sadie has lost quite a bit of weight, not that it matters. Peter fell in love with her before that. He's a great guy."

Mom shook her head. "Amazing."

Yes, Denae needed her mother out of her home. The toxicity already surrounded her like a noxious cloud, seeking to poison her thoughts, her attitudes, her entire life. She was too fragile for this. *Lord, please, help me stand my ground.*

It was a temptation to accept Michelle's invitation to have Dad intervene and keep Mom moving. But that couldn't end well. The thought of her parents in the same room, let alone Dad and Mark, was terrifying. Dad wasn't an attorney for nothing. He was confident, articulate, and wealthy, all attributes Mom hated him for. Oh, and married to the perfect woman.

No, she had to get rid of Mom on her own, before Mark arrived. But he'd come, anyway. Her blood ran cold. He was volatile. It wouldn't take much to push him over the edge.

She rubbed her fingers over her temples, trying to push back the headache that crowded in. Impossible. She stood, gathered her things, and went over to the sink before staring at her plate. She hadn't eaten since breakfast, and now half her meal remained... but how could she consume any more with the way her throat clamped and her gut roiled? As it was, she'd be lucky not to evict the little she'd swallowed.

"You're not going to eat that?"

Denae paused with her plate over the open garbage can. "I lost my appetite."

"Like you've ever had one. I'd offer to eat it, but I can't handle flavorless fish and more salad with a bland dressing."

"There are flavors!" Denae glared at her mother across the space. "Lemon and spices... and the dressing may be low-calorie, but it's got oil and vinegar and stuff."

Mom shook her head. "I don't know where I went wrong with you."

Denae opened her mouth to recite the litany then snapped it shut again. No good could come of going there.

Faint strains of music reached her ears. The folks who rented the other half of the duplex must have gotten a new CD, something other than rock. At least they usually kept the volume low, though she wouldn't complain if they turned this one up. The song was sweet and joyous. Instrumental.

And not coming from next door.

TREVOR STOOD on the sidewalk in front of Denae's house at dusk and poured his heart into the music. Second time through, now. Her RAV4 was in the driveway. Didn't that mean she was home? Unless she'd taken Poppy for a walk.

His gaze landed on an older car with Oregon plates parked at the curb. That didn't belong to the people next door. His bow faltered. Was someone visiting Denae? Was that why she'd ignored him for nearly two days, with the exception of a thank-you text for the flowers this morning? That was all the encouragement he'd received... or needed.

Maybe she was in her office, even though the kitchen and dinette lights were on. She'd never hear him from the back of upstairs. Once more through, then he'd go around and throw pebbles at her window or, you know, something drastic like ring the doorbell. But he wanted her to notice him without that.

The front door flew open, and she stood framed in the lit rectangle.

His heart stuttered, but he kept his hands moving to the beat within him as he tried to read her expression. He couldn't, not with the light behind her. She leaned against the doorframe, arms crossed, listening.

Ever singing, march we onward, victors in the midst of strife; joyful music leads us sunward in the triumph song of life.

Trevor tucked the violin and bow under his arm and bent low. When he looked at her again, someone had joined her, a heavyset woman in jeans and a gray sweatshirt. Who? What?

And then embarrassment flooded him that someone else had witnessed him pouring out his heart in serenade.

Denae stepped onto the stoop, said something to the woman, and shut the door before coming down toward him. "That's amazing, Trevor. I had no idea."

"Like it?" he asked softly. She was close enough now that he could smell her fragrance and feel the heat from her body.

She toyed with the collar of his flannel shirt, her fingertips searing his throat, making it impossible to speak. She glanced at him from only a few inches away. "I love it."

Trevor swallowed hard. "I'd like to be in your talent show. Garret will accompany me. We've gone over it like a thousand times, until my fingertips are raw." He lifted his left hand to offer the proof.

She caught his hand and traced his fingertips, and the tingling coursed through his body, sucking all the oxygen out of Montana. "I'd be honored to put you in the program."

"Thanks." *I think.*

But what was she doing to him? She let go of his hand and slid both hers around his neck. "Kiss me, cowboy," she murmured, tipping her face and tugging his closer.

He didn't need a second invitation, wrapping his free

hand around her waist and meeting her lips with his. She was sweetness and light, all the things he'd dreamed of as their lips danced together.

Trevor eased away. "I need to set the violin in its case, because this requires two hands and all my attention."

She grinned and pecked his lips. "Fair enough."

He slung his arm over her shoulder as they strolled to his truck then he tucked the violin and bow inside their case.

"So that's what was in the truck that day in Missoula."

"Yeah. I'd just bought it. It was my birthday present to myself."

Her thin eyebrows peaked. "You've only been playing such a short time?"

"Well, sort of, but not entirely. I had a couple of years of lessons when I was a kid. Until Sawyer broke my bow." He leaned against the side of the truck, away from the duplex's windows, and pulled her close. "I've ignored a lot of parts of myself."

Denae came into his arms willingly, her hands on his shoulders. She looked up at him as though realizing he had more to say.

"I don't know how to be... be a boyfriend. How to cherish someone. How to let my favorite woman fight her own battles but still be her hero."

"There are things I don't know, either."

He swept his hands up and down her back. "Like what?"

"How to eat sensibly. How to get over myself." She took a deep breath and peered at him through her eyelashes. "I'm sorry about the past couple of days. My stepmom showed up, and then my mom, and I'm behind in my work, and everything just built up. And I don't know how to process what's going on between us. How to let someone in close."

He should call her out on avoiding him, but her reasons made sense. Besides, right now, he held her in his arms. Let history remain behind them. "Close like this?" Trevor brushed his lips over hers.

She smiled, and he kissed her again. "Close... like opening my soul and letting someone see inside. I'm always afraid they'll step away when they see the real me."

"You, too?" he whispered. "But I can't imagine such a deep darkness inside you. You're a child of God, forgiven, victorious. He can certainly handle anything you and I can't."

"Truth." She sighed. "Can He handle my mother? Because she left my stepdad and showed up on my doorstep with under a quarter tank of gas in her car and cut off from her credit cards and bank accounts."

Trevor winced. "Oh, boy."

"Yeah. I don't know what to do. The situation is far too toxic for her to stay with me. Maybe I'm not a good Christian daughter, but I just can't do it. It's kind of ironic, because I'm raising money for women like her, but I don't want her around."

"Can God handle your mother? Yes. Yes, He can. I don't know how He'll do it, but I know He *can*, and He *will*, if we ask Him."

Denae rested against him, and he gathered her tight, reveling in the feel of her against him, the swish of her long hair over his arm, the way his cheek felt against the top of her head. He closed his eyes and thanked God for this moment in time then realized he did know one thing about her. She needed a man who would help her keep her focus on Jesus. He could be that man.

Trevor cleared his throat. "Almighty Father, creator of heaven and earth, You have promised where two or three are gathered in Your name, You're there in the midst of them. Well, we're here, Lord, and we have two requests for You. One, please show Denae how to handle this situation with her mom. Give her guidance. And patience. And love." He squeezed his eyes tight and his arms tighter. "My second request is for Denae and me. Lord, right now it looks to me like You might have brought us together, and I want to say thank You for that. I pray that we'll both be open to Your guidance, and that You'll show us the way forward if it's Your will. In Jesus' name, amen."

"Amen," whispered Denae, looking up at him, her eyes shining.

And Trevor kissed her again, long and slow.

CHAPTER 17

I don't know if I should take the day off, after all."
Denae stood on her doorstep, arms wrapped
around herself. "I'm so far behind since all the stuff
with my mom." The novel she was editing needed to be
turned in within just a few days, and focus had been hard
to come by.

Trevor just grinned at her from two steps down. "You
need a real day off out of Saddle Springs. As do I, now
that calving is finished and I'm transitioning back to
having a life."

Did that mean he'd want to spend more time with
her? She hoped so but was nervous at the same time. Was
she really ready for a relationship? What would happen
when Trevor caught on to all her other issues, like being a
workaholic?

He held out his hand. "Come on, woman. Get Poppy
and come. Ned Jansen called last night with just the
perfect gelding for you. You know you want to see him."

She did. But, if she bought the horse, that meant

stabling him at Standing Rock — she wouldn't get away with anywhere else — and riding regularly with Trevor. Which was good and nerve-wracking at the same time. Maybe some new scenery would lift her spirits. Trevor was right. She needed a break, and today was sunny and warm for April.

"I just need to grab my stuff and lock up." Just in case Mom came back to town from the Flying Horseshoe, or Mark arrived, or today was the day when the sleepy western town suffered its first break-in in years.

Trevor's broad smile made his dark eyes shine and the skin around them crinkle.

She could still count the number of times she'd seen him this relaxed and just plain happy. It was unbelievable to think she'd caused that. She called Poppy, grabbed the leash and her purse, and locked the door behind them. By the time she got down to the truck, Trevor had let Poppy into the backseat and was holding the passenger door open for her.

He kissed her, his lips tracing a line to her ear. "Let's have fun today."

She climbed into the tall truck then strapped her seatbelt on as Trevor closed her door and rounded the truck. Poppy raced from one side of the backseat to the other, excited for an adventure.

Once they'd pulled away from the curb, Denae reached across the console and laced her fingers with Trevor's. "Thanks for giving me a push."

He squeezed her hand. "How is your mom doing?"

"I'm thankful to the Carmichaels for taking her in and giving her a job. She complains, of course, but she has a room in the Flying Horseshoe staff bunkhouse and plenty of cabins to clean. They're open early this year with a pastoral retreat this week." The ranch was only a few miles out of town, but at least Mom was out of Denae's space.

"So she'll be surrounded by Christian pastors the whole week before Easter? She'll love that."

Denae rolled her eyes at the hint of laughter in his voice. "Whining all the way. But it's a job that comes with room and board, and she knew better than to turn it down when Amanda Carmichael made the offer. Bless Lauren for pointblank asking her mother-in-law to do it."

The truck turned onto the highway at the outskirts of Saddle Springs. Trevor glanced across the cab. "Heard anything from your stepdad?"

She shook her head. And that, right there, was the main cause of her anxiety these days. Until Mark had made his appearance and departed again — with his wife or without her — Denae simply couldn't relax. "Mom says she hasn't, either."

"Is he likely to be violent?"

"It's hard to know." Denae took in a deep breath and let it out slowly. "He could be. He always borders on aggressive, but then my mom hasn't ever really defied him before. So it's unclear what this will drive him to."

"I wish it were appropriate for you to stay with me. I'd feel better if you weren't alone, not that having your mother there was any buffer really." He cast her a side-long look, clearly troubled. "Stay with Tori or Carmen for a bit?"

She shook her head. "I need quiet to focus on work.

Besides, I can't impose on anyone like that. Tori... well, that would put me right back within Mom's daily reach. And Carmen has enough going on with Howard."

"About Howard."

Denae pressed her lips together. She hadn't meant to go there. They'd both carefully skirted the subject since date night.

"I shouldn't have spouted off about the future of the Rocking H. I don't know Howard well. He's always kept to himself and seemed to have a grudge against my family. Whether that's true or not, I can't prove, so I won't try. All I know is that the Rocking H has deteriorated at about the same rate as Eaglecrest has prospered. One big difference isn't anything anyone could foresee or change — over the generations, the Delgados tended to have a lot of boys who have ranching in their blood and have carried our family business forward."

Denae nodded. "And the Havilands haven't. Howard and his wife never had kids at all, so the future of the Rocking H isn't as secure."

"Right. Howard's oldest brother died in World War Two. Howard's twin, George, helped run the ranch for a while, but then he branched out into the rodeo business. Not participating, but in organization."

"That was Eric's grandfather, wasn't it?"

"Yes. And when Eric's parents died in that plane crash and then Eric was killed in a rodeo not long after, George passed away, too. Like he had a broken heart or something."

An entire family branch all but snuffed out, unless you

counted Juliana. And Denae was definitely counting the little girl.

"Howard's youngest brother, Bernard, moved to Dallas in the sixties and became an investment banker. He brought his grandson, Spencer, for visits sometimes in the summers, but he and Eric didn't get along all that well, even though they were close to the same age. Eric was a cocky sort who knew everything about horses, and Spencer was a city kid."

"You didn't like Eric?"

Trevor's mouth quirked to one side in a lopsided grin. "Not a lot, honestly. He was popular, and I wasn't. Girls threw themselves at him, and they didn't know I existed. Typical schoolboy stuff."

Huh. All Denae knew about Eric was from Carmen, who was definitely biased. Now she desperately wanted to know if Trevor thought Eric would have made a good ranch manager if he'd lived, but she wouldn't ask. It didn't matter, anyway. He'd died young, recklessly, leaving a widow and a toddler.

What had practical, straight-laced Carmen seen in Eric? What had he seen in her?

"I prepped out the box stall next to Ebony's last night. I know I'll have to bring the horse trailer back to Poulson if you decide you want to buy Larkspur."

Whew, Trevor was changing the subject. "I hate for you to have to make another trip. He looks good in the photos they sent, but I'm not sure. I'd always pictured getting another pinto after Juniper."

"We'll get you on him and see what you think of his

gaits. Whether you like each other. That's more important."

He was right, of course.

Trevor leaned against the metal rails next to Ned as Denae eased the gelding from a walk to a trot in the riding arena. She was a solid rider, comfortable on Larkspur. He could already envision long rides together so he could show her his favorite spots in the mountains behind Standing Rock. She could hold her own.

"She's got a good seat," Ned observed. "He came in from an older rider who didn't get out much, so he spent too much time in a stall at a boarding stable. He needs lots of exercise."

"Most horses do," Trevor agreed. "Our herd is glad to have more freedom now that the snow is melting in the high country, but having an indoor arena made all the difference the past few years. They have access to an outdoor area, too, but my brother and I have a place to give each mount a good workout."

"Heard about your spread. Eaglecrest, isn't it?"

"Yes. The riding arena is at Standing Rock, though. We bought it out a while back."

"Good of you to let your woman pick her own mount."

"She used to ride a lot as a teen, and she's picked it up again in the past year." Trevor's eyes tracked Denae as she shifted into a canter. The light on her face was worth everything. "It's time she had her own horse again, not having to make do with borrows. Not that her friends have minded."

"You can't bond that way."

Trevor nodded as Denae reined up in front of them. Larkspur tossed his head, eager to keep going. Denae ran her hand across his shoulder, and the gelding calmed. Just the opposite of what her touch did to Trevor.

Denae dismounted and led Larkspur to the gate, her gaze seeking Trevor's. "Want to check out his paces?"

He stilled. What was the right answer? Would agreeing say he didn't trust her judgment?

She grinned. "You know you want to. I think he's pretty smooth, but I value your opinion. You have way more experience than I do."

"If you really want me to." He tugged at his cowboy hat. "But I don't have any misgivings from what I observed. As far as I'm concerned, if you want him, make Ned an offer."

Ned snorted, and Trevor choked back his grin. The trader wouldn't want to do a lot of dickering, and the asking price was reasonable.

"I do want you to."

Trevor searched Denae's eyes for a few seconds before nodding. He hopped the fence and took Larkspur's reins from her before mounting up and adjusting the stirrups. He clicked his tongue, and Larkspur moved straight to a trot. He tried to focus on the horse, on the experience of moving through the paces, but part of his attention stayed on Denae and Ned talking at the railings. He half expected to see a handshake, but there wasn't one.

After three rounds of the arena, he reined in beside the gate.

Denae's eyebrows tipped upward as she met his gaze, and he nodded slightly. He couldn't discern any reason this might be a bad decision. She turned to Ned, hand outstretched. "You've got a deal."

The older man shook her hand firmly. "You won't regret it. That there's a fine horse."

Trevor dismounted and led the horse over to Denae, who slipped an apple slice to Larkspur. He munched it eagerly. Trevor turned to Ned. "I can come by Sunday afternoon with the horse trailer to pick him up, if that works for you."

"Sure. I'm not going anywhere."

Denae and Ned took care of the paperwork while Trevor surveyed the stock pens around them. It was always a temptation to pick up another horse for the family. At least, until he remembered exercising them the past couple of months after spending night shifts in the calving barn. It wasn't like they needed another mount. Kade and Cheri's kids hadn't outgrown their ponies yet, after all.

A few minutes later he opened the passenger door for Denae, pausing to drop a quick kiss to her pretty lips. Poppy, who'd stayed in the truck with the windows partway down, barked excitedly.

Denae stroked her dog. "Do you think she'll be okay around a horse?"

"I think so."

"I'm not sure I can take the time to come back with

you for Larkspur, but I hate to ask you to come alone. Maybe Ned can deliver him."

A slosh of ice water couldn't have surprised him more. "Owning a horse takes time. You'll want to come by often to ride. There are some great trails up the backend of the ranch."

"Yeah, I remember." She bit her lip, looking anywhere but at Trevor. "Maybe this was a mistake."

"No way," he said lightly. "Standing Rock's not that far out of town. It will do you good to get off your computer a bit more. Get your head into the real world." And just like that, Trevor's imagination took him to Denae moving into the large house with him. He frowned, unable to remember her ever coming up to the ranch since she'd moved back to Saddle Springs. Wasn't that strange, when she'd once lived there?

"I promise to try. You don't need to scowl."

Trevor pushed the niggle aside to mull over later. "Let's find a park and let Poppy have a run." He'd take whatever time he could get with Denae today, and maybe he could set both their insecurities to rest.

CHAPTER 18

The timber-and-stone mansion stood as tall and impressive as ever with its many arches and angles. As a preteen, Denae had imagined Dad and Michelle's house a castle with the cupola as a full-fledged turret. She'd dreamed big, back before puberty hit.

Standing Rock's grounds lay manicured and tidy, the grass turning green where it sloped away from the grand house. Nostalgia pinched hard, memories of helping Dad weed the flowerbeds before he gave up and hired a landscaping company to maintain the large property.

"When's the last time you were here?" Trevor's voice across the truck cab jerked her back to the present as he eased to a stop in front of the long, low stable. The taller arch of the riding arena where she'd practiced jumping on Juniper loomed above it at the far end, cast in deep shadow from the mountain.

She stared at the arena. She'd been twelve and spent the summer here. That had been the only time Mom had brought Mark when she came to pick Denae up. And Mark had noticed the twin buds on Denae's chest.

Her heart seized now at the memory she'd blocked. He'd caught her as she dismounted, squeezed her painfully and whispered vile promises about the fun they'd have when she filled out a little.

"The year before Dad sold it." Her voice sounded monotone, clipped, even to her.

Trying to breathe again, she tore her gaze from the hulking arena and looked across the paved circle drive and the white wooden fences to the half dozen horses grazing beyond. Two large dogs loped over from the house. Denae had left Poppy home when Trevor picked her up on his way back from Poulson with Larkspur. She'd been pushing hard to stay on top of this week's editing project. She couldn't let her client down, not even if it meant letting Trevor make the trip by himself. He'd volunteered, after all.

"Probably looks just the same." Trevor's forearms rested on the steering wheel as he watched her.

"I mostly saw it in the middle of summer. Roses in bloom, not daffodils. Dad loves roses." Her voice echoed as from a deep cavern.

Trevor winced. "Some of those winter-killed a couple of years ago when we had a harsh cold snap before the snow came."

Figured. She forced a smile. "Nothing stays the same, does it?"

"Do we want it to?"

"Sometimes." Not that she wanted to be a kid on the cusp of puberty again, but life had been so much simpler before Mark noticed her. "This ranch was my anchor. My only happy place." Until it wasn't.

She hadn't expected the buried memory to assault her the first time she saw Standing Rock again. Of course, she'd known this was where Trevor lived. She'd even imagined him rambling around in that giant house. But it all seemed tinged with darkness now. As soon as she remembered Mark.

"Are you okay?" He sounded concerned.

Real life guys weren't sensitive, so it must be a fluke. Mark was anything but, and he was raising his sons to be just like himself. Dad was a whole lot nicer, but clueless without Michelle to interpret for him. Only men in romance novels were truly perceptive. Written by delusional women, naturally.

She shook her head. No, that wasn't true. Kade treated Cheri with respect. James was head over heels for Lauren. And it wasn't just because those couples' love was fresh and new. Look at the senior Delgados. Russ and Gloria cooked together — when Ruthie allowed them in the kitchen — and worked together on the ranch. James and Tori's parents seemed to have a great working relationship, too, even with Bill's disability.

Denae wanted to think it was because those women had never experienced life the way she had, but then there was Cheri—

Trevor's hand squeezed her arm. "You're scaring me. You look like you've seen a ghost."

She pushed out a tremulous smile and reached for the door handle. "Let's get Larkspur settled." Could she go even that far into the stable without the darkness flooding her?

"Still up for a short ride? Even just a few rounds of the arena to give you and Larkspur a chance to bond."

Anywhere but the arena. "Not tonight. I'm not feeling really well."

"A horse under my backside and the smell of cotton-wood sap does wonders to make me feel better."

That sounded so... Trevor. But she needed out of here. She could edit a couple of more chapters this evening, and Poppy needed another walk. "Maybe tomorrow." Then she'd have to think of something else.

He bit his lip as he studied her face, and she offered him a tremulous smile before shoving the truck door open. "I'll get that..."

But she was already on the pavement, pushing the door closed, striding toward the back of the horse trailer. She grabbed the lever bar and swung it out of the way, pulling the door open before Trevor stood beside her, tossing her an inscrutable look as he stepped inside to guide Larkspur out.

Well, maybe she could figure out that expression if she tried, but not right now. She was pushing him away. Again. She knew it, but how could she stop herself? How could she trust him? Not this easily. Not with Mark all but leering over her shoulder.

The two large dogs sat on either side of her as Trevor backed Larkspur out.

She fumbled for the piece of apple from her pocket but couldn't find it before Trevor led the gelding into the stable and into the first large box stall. Whew. Trevor unbuckled the halter in one fluid motion, then measured a scoop of grain into the feeder, talking to him the entire time.

Denae trailed behind. Whose horse was this, anyway? Hers, but Trevor acted like Larkspur was his. Just because she had less experience and held back a little? What was she supposed to do, just stand in the alleyway and watch? But getting in there meant getting close to Trevor, giving and receiving kisses as though nothing was wrong. Pretending her confidence hadn't taken a dive a minute in the past few days.

KEEPING HIS BACK TO DENAE, Trevor caressed the chestnut's head. What was going on with her? How could a guy keep putting himself out there when he never knew if she was going to be hot or cold? Who needed that drama? Maybe she was like Meg, after all. Keeping a man off balance then offering no substance once she had his attention. If he wasn't a challenge, he wasn't worth having around.

Denae had refused to return to Poulson with him, citing deadlines. Now she didn't want to ride her new acquisition, and it didn't sound legit. Lack of eye contact was a dead giveaway.

Lord, what am I supposed to do here? I've fallen in love with her, and she's pulling away, and I feel helpless to stop her. It's like Meg all over again.

The gelding whiffled in his ear, soft, warm, and moist. He couldn't help smiling, just a little. At least horses always loved a man. And the dogs. He could count on Ranger and Mickey. He'd closed himself off since Meg. Tried to convince himself that the ranch was enough. Horses, dogs, cattle. His parents and brothers.

Watching Kade tilt toward romance over and over had been excruciating to watch. Everything in Trevor screamed at his brother to protect himself. Sometimes the words had even come out, but Kade was the trusting sort, and it had worked out in the end.

And Trevor was back on the outside looking in after daring to dream in the past few weeks. Denae *wasn't* like Meg. His head knew that, but his heart only saw the similarities. Unlike five years ago, Trevor was seeking God's will. He wasn't a hormonally-driven fool playing blindly with fire this time.

But Denae had so many issues he didn't understand, and couldn't, if she didn't let him into the inner workings of her mind. Was she just as afraid as he was?

The thought froze his hands on Larkspur's neck.

That couldn't be right. She'd always seemed so confident until lately. Until her mother had shown up on her doorstep, right when Denae was working with the arts council to help fund a safe house for victims of domestic violence.

Why? It was a great venture, sure, but why had Denae taken it on? For her mother? Or... because she had experience of her own?

He pivoted toward the stall door, but Denae wasn't there. He patted the gelding once more and murmured something to him then strode out of the box, clicking the gate behind him, and out toward the truck.

Denae sat on the grass beside the driveway, Mickey's head in her lap while Ranger leaned over her shoulder. Her long hair obscured her face.

Trevor crouched beside her and brushed a few strands over her shoulder. "Hey," he said softly. "Talk to me."

Her head shook slightly, and her fingers dug into Mickey's neck fur.

"We've got something going, Denae. Something good. But it's nothing without communication."

She didn't move a muscle, so Trevor plunked down beside her, nudging Ranger out of the way. He wrapped his arm around her shoulders, but she stayed stiff against him.

"I need to go home, Trevor," she said at last. Her voice was quiet yet firm.

"We were going to go for a ride and then out to The Branding Iron for dinner." Which was why she'd ridden out with him in the truck in the first place, since he was returning to Saddle Springs anyway.

"I can't."

"Can't... or won't?" As soon as his words hit the sound waves, Trevor regretted them. But it was true. Something in her was pushing him away.

She surged to her feet, and Mickey bounded up beside her, gazing up in adoration. "Does it matter? Please take me home."

"It does matter." He stayed seated, forearms resting on his splayed knees. "Because apparently I've done something wrong, and I honestly don't know what." He hadn't mentioned anorexia lately, or Carmen, or anything he knew might set her off.

Denae glanced at him then away. "It's not you. It's me."

Classic brush-off line, and one he thought he'd never hear. Not when he'd been so cautious to commit in the first place, waiting until he was sure. There'd been nothing but interest visible in her for the past year. Until they'd started dating.

Trevor angled his cowboy hat back and watched her closely. "I'm sure it's more complex than that."

She bit her lip. "Being here at Standing Rock triggered a lot of... a lot of negative memories I didn't expect. This was a mistake."

His heart seized. "What kind of mistake?" Was she talking about him, specifically, or on the ranch in general? But neither answer made sense. Neither was welcome.

"Having you board Larkspur here. I should have talked to Garret. Canyon Crossing Stables is a lot closer to town. Handier."

"But then you'd be spending all your time with Garret, not me."

Denae winced slightly.

Oh, man, *so* not a good sign. "We're the ones who are dating, Denae. We're the ones who are moving forward in a relationship. At least, that's what I thought was happening."

She sucked in her lips, looking anywhere but at him.

Trevor clambered to his feet and stood in front of her. He tipped her chin up, but she wouldn't meet his gaze. "Did you have other plans? Like to see if you could get me out of my shell and then dump me because you'd accomplished your goal? Just tell me now if that's all I mean to you, because you won. I care about you. A lot. Stomp on me if you must, and let's get it over with."

"That's not what it is, Trevor." She pulled away and shook off his hands. "I told you. It's me. I have commitment issues."

He stepped closer as she backed away. "You're the one always spouting romance stuff at everyone. Who said commitment came easy? I bet no one, ever. We all want to protect ourselves from hurt." Some more than others, like men who'd had their heart broken once before. Like men who'd watched their brother go through hell and back, not once, but twice. Only the third time had it really been worth it, and that didn't make up for the previous agony, did it? Nope. No matter what Kade said.

Denae's arms wrapped around her thin middle. Classic self-defense.

He took another step closer. She shifted back until her shoulders hit the fence. Her eyes flared for a brief instant. Fear? She was afraid of him? What on earth?

Trevor moved closer and grasped her upper arms. Gently. "I won't hurt you, Denae. I never could. Whatever you're afraid of, it isn't me. Whatever the reason you're forcing me away, it isn't because I've pushed you too hard." It couldn't be, but he couldn't help second guessing with the rug being yanked out from beneath his feet.

"I'm not afraid of you."

"Then look at me."

Her gaze ricocheted off his. Trevor's hands tightened a microscopic amount. He hadn't meant to, but somehow he needed to get her attention. He leaned in and captured her mouth with his, but her lips didn't soften. He pushed a little harder, fueled by frustration, by a desperate need to remind her what they had together.

Two hands shoved at his chest, and he stumbled back a step.

"Trevor, don't."

"Don't what? Don't remind you we have an actual relationship?" The words came out louder and more bitter than he'd intended. He hadn't intended any of the last five minutes. The last half hour. How had things gotten out of hand so quickly?

"We don't. We can't." Denae's face was flushed, whether from anger or something else, he couldn't tell. "Take me home, Trevor. Please. Right now, or I'll call someone to come get me."

All fight fizzled into flatness. He'd done the wrong thing. Again. And this time he'd lost her.

CHAPTER 19

E diting romance was the stupidest job Denae could ever have come up with. Every flowery turn of phrase, every fluttering eyelash, and especially every swoon-worthy kiss caused her to shoot away from her treadmill desk with the impulse to bang her head against a brick wall. It was all she could do not to fill the manuscript's sidebar with comment after vitriolic comment about the characters' thoughts, actions, and dialogue.

And this was one of her favorite authors, a consistent bestseller with over a dozen novels to her name. Fans clamored for her next story, and Denae had always been smugly silent about getting to read and have advance input on each new addition to the series.

Today it all seemed like horse feed, which was also not a helpful train of thought. She needed to make some decisions about Larkspur, but not now. Now she must push through the final chapters of the manuscript and endure the starry eyes and romantic proposal and the passionate kisses that would seal this imaginary couple's happily-ever-after.

Fiction. Happily-ever-after was nothing but hyped-up fables, and she'd helped perpetuate and perfect that myth over and over. No wonder so many eyebrows hiked up when she announced her profession. They knew what she'd been too blind in her unicorn-and-rainbows world to admit. Romance was nothing but a delusion that pretended to be more, like Oz's wizard.

It wasn't even all Trevor's fault, no matter how much she longed to shove every speck of blame onto his broad, muscular shoulders. Even though that last kiss yesterday had not been sweet and loving. It had been more of a warning, and one she would heed. She'd pushed him, and he'd responded. He was only a man, and she'd found the limit of his tolerance.

The doorbell rang downstairs, and she turned toward the staircase and glared. The only person who would dare break into her working time had better be the FedEx driver delivering the box of books promised by one of her authors. She had an entire bookcase loaded with the works she'd edited. She might as well donate them all to the new safe house. Not that those women needed their heads full of twaddle any more than Denae did.

The bell chimed again, and Poppy barked. Denae tried to shove her foul mood aside as she jogged down the stairs and over to the door. She looked through the peep-hole only to discover, not the FedEx man, but Cheri Delgado.

She didn't want to open the door, but Cheri would have heard her footsteps on the tiles. She couldn't be that rude to the woman married to Trevor's brother. What was Cheri doing here? Either she knew what happened last night or she didn't. Either way, this was awkward.

Cheri smiled at her, the lines of her face serene. Her hands cradled her belly, a huge protrusion with the baby due soon. "Hey, Denae. Can I come in for a few? I could sure use a cup of tea before I head back up to Eaglecrest. I know you usually work mornings, but I wanted to bring the painting for the silent auction while I was in town."

Denae knew she looked a mess. She'd been up most of the night and hadn't had a shower yet today. Her yoga pants and baggy sweatshirt were likely creased. Maybe even stinky.

Cheri waited, the smile firmly in place, the framed artwork leaning against her leg.

"Come on in." It wasn't like she'd been accomplishing anything on the stupid manuscript anyway. And Cheri might as well hear the story from Denae as from Trevor, since the friendly expression wouldn't last long once she knew. Denae led the way into the small kitchen. "I'll put the kettle on. What brings you into town without the kids?"

"Kade's mom kept them since I had an appointment with the obstetrician. It's so much easier not to drag the two of them with me everywhere, especially when there are pelvic exams to look forward to." Cheri set the painting against the wall where Poppy sniffed it.

"Makes sense. How's everything with the baby?" Denae filled the kettle and set it on the stovetop before turning to Cheri.

"Good. He's in position but hasn't dropped into the birth canal yet. Taking his sweet time."

"It's a boy?" Of course it was. The Delgados ran to boys, and Denae had just made sure she never carried one. Didn't matter. She probably couldn't get pregnant anyway, since all the recent stresses had kept her menses at bay. She was a mess. A mess the Delgados didn't deserve, especially Trevor.

Cheri ran her hand over the baby as she settled into one of the chairs by the tiny table. "So they say. We're ready for him."

"That's great."

"Trevor says you bought a horse from Ned Jansen. That's so exciting."

Any lingering doubt about what Cheri knew dissipated. "I did." Deep breath. "I need to give Garret a call and see about boarding Larkspur at Canyon Crossing, though. It's so much closer to town."

Cheri's eyebrows shot up into her side-swept bangs. "Why would you do that?"

Denae turned to pull two mugs out of the cupboard. "Trevor and I... I just can't."

"Can't what, sweetie?"

"He deserves better."

"I've never seen Trevor happier than in the past couple of months. He's in love with you, if I don't miss my guess."

Yeah, he'd seemed happy. Denae probably had, too, but it had been destined to fail. She stared into the cupboard, the labels on all the boxes of tea swimming together.

"What happened?" Cheri's voice remained gentle.

Denae grabbed a box, snapped the cupboard door shut, and rescued the boiling water. "It doesn't matter."

"Pretty sure it does. To you. To Trevor. To everyone who loves either one of you."

She took a deep breath. "Romance is an illusion."

"It's not. Kade is the kindest, most patient and loving person I've ever known."

"Have you forgotten the years where you feared that Harmony's father would find you? You ended up in shelters like the one we're trying to start here."

"I haven't forgotten. Dillon's still a mean person. At least he got tired of being a father and demanding time with Harmony and left town again. It's a whole lot easier when he sweeps in for occasional visits than when he's in our faces claiming his rights every week." Cheri caught Denae's gaze. "But that doesn't negate Kade's love for me and Harmony both. It doesn't negate the safety and trust and thankfulness I feel every single day."

"That's great."

"And Trevor is a lot like Kade. When he commits, it will be one hundred twenty percent. He will be all in with the woman he loves, supporting her, nurturing her, believing in her, adoring her."

Denae blinked back burning tears. "You're probably right, but only if the woman deserves that devotion. I hope he finds her."

"I think he already did."

The tea had steeped long enough. Denae squeezed out the teabags and offered one cup to Cheri. "I have honey, but no cream. Sorry about that."

"Honey would be good, thanks." Cheri spooned a bit into her tea. "I've been rather curious why you chose to support the safe house here in town. I know why it's important more than most, mind you, but is it because of your mom?" She pinned Denae with a look. "Or something more personal?"

"Uh..." Whoa. Denae hadn't expected that question. Her hands trembled as she set the cup back on the counter.

"You don't have to tell me, of course, but it seems you might need a friend."

"I can't believe you're saying that when Trevor and I are over. You should be on his side."

Cheri lifted the mug and had a sip. "If you have another Christian friend to confide in, that's great. Or a counselor."

"Oh, I've got a full psych team at my disposal." Denae spit the words out. "I've got more issues than anyone wants to face, especially me."

There was silence for a long moment. "Are you suicidal?"

All she wanted was for Cheri to leave. Now. But there was no way she could wrestle a large pregnant woman out the door, and there was no way Trevor's sister-in-law was going to budge any minute soon. "Occasionally," she let out. "Not recently."

"You're worth so much. Jesus gave Himself for you."

"I know that." Denae tapped her temple. "I know a lot of things, but it doesn't always help. There are other voices, like my stepdad's."

"He says you're worthless?" Cheri's words were so quiet Denae almost missed them.

She nodded, a short, hard nod. "Worth building up like a house of cards and knocking down. Worth being an outlet for his aggression. Worth mocking."

"Oh, sweetie."

"I don't blame Mom for leaving him. She should have done it years ago. She should never have gotten mixed up with him in the first place, but I guess having all his attention riveted on her — at least for a while — was enticing after my father nearly totally ignored her during the short time they were together. He lived for work." Like she did.

"So your stepdad's attention wandered?"

Denae laughed bitterly. "Did it ever. Anything in a skirt. Always playing. Always manipulating. Always controlling."

"Did he sexually abuse you?"

She froze. "He likes his women rounder."

Cheri studied her. "That clears up a lot of things."

"Does it?" Oh, Denae knew it did. She could look back and see the patterns. Not only that, she could pinpoint exactly when things started souring with Trevor. It wasn't about Carmen, not really. It wasn't about the lack of a goodnight kiss.

It was about Mom showing up on her doorstep, and Mark's ugly shadow looming over the both of them. Everything he'd done, everything he'd said surged over her as though she were that girl again. Every bit of progress she'd made with countless therapists, nutritionists, and psychologists faded away.

She hadn't seen Mark in almost four years except for

at Grandma Essery's funeral. She'd managed to avoid him then, but the power he had over her flooded back as strong as ever. She'd never be free of his influence.

Never.

MICKEY BARKED, and Ranger joined in.

Trevor set the pitchfork on a hook and strode to the stable door, blinking against the sudden brightness.

A vintage red pickup towing a horse trailer had pulled up beside the stable, and Garret Morrison stepped out with a broad smile.

Maybe Trevor could wipe that thing right off the young punk's face. He glowered at Garret. "Hey."

"Hey backatcha. Denae asked me to come pick up Larkspu—"

"No."

Garret lifted his hat and scratched his head. "He's her horse?"

"Yes."

"Well, then..."

"I'm not letting you take him unless she tells me herself."

Garret's eyes narrowed. "She said she wants to board him closer to town. I'm not trying to steal him, man."

Maybe he wasn't trying to steal the horse, but how about the woman? "Sorry you wasted your time coming up here."

"Phone her."

Like she'd pick up. He'd called several times. Left a

message apologizing for kissing her like that with all his frustration showing. It definitely hadn't helped his cause... which had been lost before that. How? Who knew. But lost.

Trevor pulled his phone from his pocket and tapped her number. It rang once, twice, three times, then clicked over to voicemail. "Hey, it's Trevor." Like she didn't know. "Garret's here with some stupid story about taking Larkspur. Call me."

One.

Two.

Three.

His phone rang. Well, there went that vague and obviously unfounded theory that she hadn't noticed his previous calls. "Trevor here." He turned and strode down the driveway with the cell to his ear. Away from Garret.

"Hey, sorry I forgot to call. Yeah, I've been super busy and asked Garret to swing by."

"You can't do this, Denae. We had an agreement." They'd once agreed on so much more.

"I'm sorry?"

"Are you?" Silence. "Because *I* am. I still have no idea what I did wrong. Yes, I reacted badly yesterday evening, and I'm truly sorry for that. But before that. Can you fill me in?"

"Trevor, please don't."

"Don't what? Did I imagine everything? I'm pretty sure I didn't. I've never had a vivid imagination. Not like you." As hard as he tried, he couldn't keep a hint of bitterness out of his voice. He'd been blindsided. First by love, then by rejection.

"No." Her voice softened. "I don't think you imagined everything. I keep telling you, it's not your fault. Please believe me."

"Here's the thing, Denae. I hear those words and, yes, they make sense. But don't you see? You're in my heart. It's impossible not to feel the hurt. Being absolved doesn't change anything." Maybe it did. How should he know? He was trying to strategize with the cards he'd been dealt, but he didn't understand what game she played. It was like trying to play with Jericho. His three-year-old nephew invented new rules every time.

But this game was for keeps.

And there seemed no way to win when the rules kept shifting.

CHAPTER 20

Denae slowed her pace as she read back through her comments on the latest edit, deleting some of her most cryptic criticism. It was hard to evaluate objectively, but she knew this author and couldn't afford to lose her.

Her hands stilled on the keyboard. What if she'd completely lost her touch? If she didn't believe in romance anymore, was she washed up as an editor? Maybe she should switch to some other genre. Thrillers, maybe.

As if.

She stopped the treadmill and stared out the second-story window. There was that half-completed degree in interior design. She could go back to school and finish it off. Get into a world where women were too busy with their high-powered careers to worry about romance. Women like her stepmom, who was a sought-after IT consultant. Except Michelle loved Dad, so never mind her.

Denae crafted a polite email, resisting the overwhelming urge to over-apologize for her harsh edits, attached the document, and hit send just as someone pounded on the door downstairs.

Poppy howled and yelped.

Denae froze. That was no polite knock or doorbell ring. She hurried down the hall and peeked out of the spare room window. Her gut froze at the sight of the older pickup blocking her RAV4 into the driveway.

Mark.

And she was home alone.

She'd known he would come. Mom's trail hadn't been particularly subtle and, even if it had, Mark still would have assumed the correct destination. Okay, so how could she get rid of him? Just give him directions to the Flying Horseshoe? Did Mom deserve that?

At least Denae could give her mother warning, which was more than she'd had. But that wasn't fair to the Carmichael family, whose ranch resort was full up this week. They didn't need all the drama.

Poppy howled again as Denae knelt on the chest in front of the window and peered at the thinning hair on top of Mark's head. He paced the stoop with quick jerky steps then pounded on the door again. Any second now he'd try the knob.

She'd locked it. She always did. Force of habit from living in the city and knowing she got too immersed in her work to stay aware.

It wouldn't stop Mark, though. He could likely kick through that in two tries, and she'd be trapped. There was no escape from the duplex without going out either the front door or the back patio door, but where could she go? And would Poppy stay quiet as they escaped?

Not likely.

Denae fingered her phone. Trevor would come, but he was at least twenty minutes out of town. Besides, she'd broken up with him, remember? Even Garret was too far away and had no real reason to come to her rescue, anyway.

Pastor Roland. He was on the planning team for the safe house.

She hit his contact button just as Mark's size-twelve work boot jammed into the door right beside the knob.

Poppy barked like a crazed and cornered beast.

Mark stepped back and came at the door again.

TREVOR LIFTED his great grandfather's violin to his shoulder. He was in no mood for *Ode to Joy*, that was for sure. All the hope he'd felt two months ago — two days ago — had melted along with the last of the snow in the shadowed spots behind the arena.

Ashokan Farewell, the haunting theme song for Ken Burns' miniseries about the Civil War, came to mind.

Trevor drew his bow across the old strings, absorbing the sad lyrics of lost love. Perfect. He'd still play in the talent night next week — he'd given his word, and he wouldn't go back on it — but he reserved the right to play something as mournful and woebegone as he felt. He worked through it again seeking alternate fingering here and there, making the arrangement his own. *Focus, Trevor, focus.*

He didn't want to think about Denae. Didn't want to think about how he'd cleaned out Larkspur's box stall this afternoon, the one the gelding had inhabited for less than twenty-four hours. Didn't want to think about the other horses that needed exercising, the fact that he needed to start fieldwork soon, that Kade would be distracted — again — by the birth of his son any day now, that Sawyer had vetoed the family photo shoot, so Trevor wouldn't have to.

He forced his mind back to the music, choosing which notes to hold, which to accelerate. Feeling the emotional separation in the lyrics.

The bow scraped discordantly. Ranger's head jerked up, and he gave a low growl.

Yeah. Trevor knew how it sounded, too. Just like it felt. He set the instrument on his desk beside the unlit fireplace and paced into the other room. How long would it take to get over Denae? He had a bad track record. It had taken five years to get over Meg, and he'd only been in unresolved lust with her.

Trevor loved Denae. He hadn't even had a chance to tell her, not that it likely would have changed anything.

He, Trevor Russel Delgado, was in love, and the object of his affection — no, his passion — had cut him off. He had a choice. Accept her verdict or stick his neck out and try to win her back. But, how, when he didn't know what he'd done in the first place?

It's not you. It's me.

She'd said that several times. Could it be true? Did

she think she was unlovable? The truth of that thought settled into his heart. Underneath it all, she did believe that.

If he was going to convince her otherwise, he had his work cut out for himself. He needed to be sure he could follow through. That he could love her forever, because if he chose this route, there was no offramp. Ever. How could he convince her she was worthy of love?

Then there was the flip side. After Meg, he'd never dreamed of finding love. Never planned to marry and have a family. Coming back for more after heartbreak was for optimistic saps like Kade. Trevor was smarter than his brother. He'd vowed never to put himself in a woman's hands again and let her control his happiness.

But that wasn't what was happening here. It wasn't about him. He wanted to bring joy and freedom and love to Denae. He wanted to protect her and grow together in the Lord beside her. He wanted to share secret smiles with her like those between Kade and Cheri.

Trevor stared out the breakfast room's bay window at the prickly stubs of Stewy Archibald's prized rosebushes in the garden outside. They looked dead, but it was only the end of April. They needed warm sunshine and spring rains. The landscaping company had pruned them recently, removing the deadwood to offer the soon-to-form buds the best possible chance at filling their area of influence with beauty and fragrance.

He'd send roses. Flowers had broken her silence once before. The internet would tell him what color and how many then he'd phone Florabelle.

And he'd take this risk. It was everything on the line for Denae.

Whatever it took. Lord, help him.

DENAE STOOD GLUED to her peephole, one hand clutching Poppy's leash and the other on the knob as she watched her stepfather charge her door for the fourth time. Miraculously, the deadbolt had held, but it was a cheapie, designed to keep an honest man honest, not for this sort of onslaught. She wasn't going to let Mark burst in on her. Wasn't going to let him touch a finger to her or wreck her home.

Now.

She twisted the knob and jerked out of the way as his shoulder slammed into the door. The force of his momentum carried him deep inside where he tripped over the step stool she'd left in his path and crashed to the ceramic floor.

Denae yanked Poppy out the door and darted for the RAV4. She threw the dog inside, jammed the key into the ignition, and shoved it into reverse. She slammed into Mark's truck, but the rear tire carrier on her SUV absorbed most of the impact. At least to *her* vehicle. She shoved the gear shift into drive, yanked on the steering wheel, and stomped on the accelerator just as Mark careened down the steps in front of the SUV, clamping his right hand over his left wrist. She didn't want to run him over, but she couldn't stop fast enough.

He dove out of her way as she wrenched the wheel

hard to her left. Somewhere in the recesses of her mind she heard his yelled obscenities, so he must be okay. Ish.

Sirens screamed from a few blocks away as her vehicle bumped off the curb and lurched to a stop on the street. Pastor Roland said he'd call 9-1-1, but that he'd be right over as well.

Somehow, she hadn't thought of calling the police. She should have, but she wasn't used to Mark actually crossing the line. He was usually much more careful than this.

He'd started for her vehicle until he heard the sirens. Then he shot her a venomous glare and lumbered toward his truck.

Not on my watch, buddy. She slammed the RAV4 into reverse and rammed his truck again, pushing it several yards down the block.

Seconds later a police cruiser angle parked at the other end of the truck, hemming it in. The siren shut off in mid-wail, leaving space in the sudden silence to hear Mark's vocabulary turning the air blue.

Pastor Roland jogged around the corner of the block, heaving for oxygen as he approached the window Denae cracked open. "Are you okay?"

"I'm fine. Thanks for calling the police." Her shaking hands belied her words as she turned off the ignition. "And for coming."

"An intruder breaking down a door is a matter for the police, not a middle-aged overweight pastor."

"I'm sorry. I didn't even think."

"I'm honored." He poked his head toward the truck,

where the officer snapped handcuffs on Mark's wrists. "But *that's* what needed to happen."

Denae let out a long breath as she sagged against her steering wheel. Poppy tried to wiggle into her lap, but there was no room. "I don't want to live through something like that ever again."

"I'm sure." Roland opened her door. "I think the officer will need you to make a statement. I'll stay with you." He reached for her arm and steadied her as she slid out, leaving Poppy whining inside.

Mark surged toward her, eyes crazed. "Where is Lisa?"

The officer's gun whipped out. "Stop it right there."

"She's hiding my wife from me."

"My mother left you because you're an adulterous violent jerk, but she's not here."

"You're lying." He spat at her feet. Missed.

"All right. Into the car, buster. You need a cool down."

Mark let out a string of expletives.

Because that was going to make the officer more lenient. Right.

The policeman pushed Mark into the cruiser's backseat and shut the door. "Can you come down to the station, Ms. Archibald? We need a statement from you. And the wife he mentioned... your mother? Is she available?"

"I can call and ask her to come into town. She's working at the Flying Horseshoe."

"I'd appreciate that." He tipped his cap in her direction. "He's got some anger issues. Maybe we can get to the bottom of it." He climbed into the cruiser and drove away, Mark glaring from the rear window.

Still quaking, Denae dropped to the curb. "Can he be charged here for what happened in Oregon?"

Pastor Roland lowered himself beside her. "That attempt at break and enter was right here in Montana, Denae."

"But he didn't. I opened the door."

"Good thinking, to escape that way, but there's a solid boot-print with his name on it over on the door. I'd say that spells intent." He chuckled. "You should give your mom a call."

"Yeah." Denae thumbed on her phone, tapped her mom's contact info, and asked her to meet at the duplex as soon as possible. Mom was stronger than she had been, because she agreed. Maybe this time she'd cut all ties with Mark, and he'd face his consequences.

Poppy ran back and forth in the SUV's backseat, barking.

"I should let her out." But Denae stayed on the edge of the curb. She was exhausted. This, on top of everything that had happened the past week, had drained all her energy. Wooziness threatened to pull her under.

When had she last eaten? She'd been so worked up about Trevor and then the manuscript, she couldn't remember if she'd had anything since lunch yesterday. Could that even be possible? More than twenty-four hours?

Denae staggered to her feet. "I need... something to eat."

The pastor cast her a worried glance. "I'll get your dog, if you think she'd be okay with me."

"Sure." The walk up the sidewalk, up the few steps, and into the duplex seemed to take forever. Denae tugged the fridge open and blinked at the contents. A bag of salad mix. A cucumber. Celery. Half a grilled chicken breast.

Was this really what her life had come to? No wonder people worried about her.

"Here, let me fix someth—" Pastor Roland's voice cut off as he leaned toward the fridge. "Denae, you need something real. You sit down. I'll be right back." He turned aside and spoke into his phone, so quickly and quietly she couldn't quite catch the words. A moment later he returned. "Bonnie will be right over with some soup. She made a big batch of beef barley this morning."

"She doesn't need to." The protest sounded weak even to Denae. She sagged into a chair at her kitchen table, Poppy crowding her legs.

"I think she does." He took the other chair. "Do you want to talk? You're not just naturally thin, are you?"

She shook her head. Tired. So tired. Maybe after she'd slept for a week she could face this nightmare. She'd come clean publicly once before, and she could do it again. She couldn't keep running. Couldn't keep hurting people. People like Trevor. Couldn't keep pretending she was fine when she wasn't.

The doorbell rang, and Pastor Roland rose. "You stay right here. Bonnie's quicker than I thought." He opened the door and came back with a large bouquet of roses, which he set on the table between them with a grin. "For you. I guess the soup will still be a few minutes."

The roses were gorgeous. A dozen red ones with three white ones tucked among them. Red for love. White for purity. Fifteen for apology. Did Trevor know all that? Because the arrangement couldn't be from anyone else.

Her hand shook as she tugged the card out and fragrance filled the air. She was tired of her hands trembling. She wasn't taking good care of herself. Things needed to change.

Please forgive me. I love you. Trevor

Tears burned her eyes. Things like how she treated Trevor needed to change. She didn't deserve him, but he was still here, offering his love in the most romantic, storybook way.

She texted her thanks.

CHAPTER 21

A shabby truck with Oregon plates sat in front of Denae's place with her RAV4 jammed against its grille. Somebody had done a terrible job at parking.

Trevor made a U-turn, parked across the street, and hopped out, giving a longer look at the two vehicles mashed together. That had been no accident. Why had her stepfather rammed the SUV? Looked like the frame of her rear tire carrier was bent.

Her texts had been cryptic. Thanks for the flowers then a note that Mark had arrived and was in police custody. That she and her mother needed to go to the station and file statements against him.

Not without Trevor by her side. With another side-long look at the two vehicles, he strode across the street and up the sidewalk. He tapped on the door, noticing a large boot print beside the knob.

His blood went cold. Denae hadn't said much about her stepfather, but a man who tried to break down a door wasn't someone to trifle with. *He's in custody. He can't hurt her.*

Pastor Roland opened the door. "Trevor. Nice choice in flowers."

Trevor blinked. "Uh, hello to you, too, pastor."

"Come on in. Denae's just having a bite to eat while we wait for her mom to arrive."

"You... what are you doing here?" It may not have been the most polite way to ask, but everything was off kilter. A crazed man had tried to break into Denae's home, and Trevor hadn't been here to protect her. Had Pastor Roland? Why?

"She called me while he was trying to break down the door. I called 9-1-1 and hurried over, but the police were quicker." Pastor Roland's gaze sharpened on Trevor. "She nearly passed out. Not from panic or excitement so much as that she hadn't eaten."

Trevor closed his eyes for an instant. Was he really, *really* up for this? Yes. He and God had gone over this part.

"Bonnie brought over some hot soup. Want a bowl?"

"Uh, no. Thanks, but I had lunch a couple of hours ago. I'm good." He took a step forward, hoping the man would retreat. He wanted to see Denae. Let his own eyes determine if she was all right.

"Can I talk to you for a moment, son?"

Trevor shifted on his feet, peering past the man. Denae needed him, but it was the pastor she'd called. Why?

"It's important."

"Okay, fine. Make it quick."

Pastor Roland came out on the stoop, pulling the door shut behind him. He took a seat on the top step and patted the space next to him.

Trevor sat, removing his cowboy hat and turning it over and over.

"I'm going to let Denae tell you everything that happened, or you'll hear it in her deposition. If you're coming to the station."

What kind of man did the pastor think he was? "Absolutely."

"My advice to you is that you pray very carefully about this relationship if you choose to move forward. Denae comes across as very bubbly and vivacious, but underneath is a young woman who's quite insecure."

Trevor pulled to his feet. "Thank you, pastor. I know that. We've talked about it." Not as much as they were going to have to, and soon, but still. "We all have some insecurities. Some bury it deeper than others. And I don't say that to make light of Denae."

The older man angled his head and looked up at Trevor. "Bonnie and I will be praying for you both."

"Thanks." Trevor opened the door and strode inside. The rose bouquet all but hid the woman seated on the other side of the table. The woman he loved. "Denae?"

The pastor's wife rose from her chair. "Good to see you, Trevor. I'll give you a moment. We're expecting Lisa any time now."

"Thanks." He'd been saying that a lot, but maybe that meant he had years of taking things for granted to make up for. He rounded the table and knelt beside Denae's chair, reaching for her hands.

She laid her spoon into a soup bowl and turned toward him, her hair wisping out of its long braid, her dark eyes large and luminous.

"Denae."

She grasped his hands and seemed to be peering through his eyes and into his soul. "Do you mean it?"

Mean what? His brain scrambled before his gaze caught on the Florabelle card beside her spoon.

Please forgive me. I love you. Trevor

Not his handwriting, but his sentiment in every word. "I love you, Denae. I'm sorry I keep messing up. I don't mean to hurt you, but I probably will again sometime because I'm human, and I've never traveled this path before. I'll make mistakes. I'll miss cues. I'll get tired and impatient and crabby."

Was her gaze softening any? Was that a hint of a smile at the corners of her mouth?

He pushed on. "I may not be an expert on romance. I've even been somewhat cynical about it. Well, I guess that's obvious..."

Denae tilted her head slightly, definitely with a teensy grin.

"But I'm willing to learn. With you. For you. Because you are the greatest treasure God has ever brought into my life, and you are worth it."

"I have an apology to make, too."

Trevor stretched closer and brushed his lips over hers. "No, you don't. It was all me."

"Not all." She pushed back a little, her dark eyes serious.

He couldn't think of a thing.

"It's about Carmen. It wasn't fair to you, me dumping all that on you and expecting you to instantly agree with me. And then getting upset with you when you didn't."

"You had some valid points."

"But I didn't handle it well… and then sending Garret out for Larkspur. Seeing the ranch again spiraled me into nightmares I'd totally blocked. I just—"

"Oh, my goodness, Denae, are you all right? I can't believe—" Lisa's voice cut off. "Excuse me."

Trevor rocked back on his heels and rose, tugging Denae up with him. A glance in her bowl showed only a bit of rich brown broth remaining with a few kernels of barley floating in it. She'd eaten then. That was the most important part. The story could wait.

Denae tumbled into her mother's arms, and the two clung together, rocking. "I'm so sorry," cried Lisa, over and over.

After a long moment, Pastor Roland spoke. "Are we ready to go over to the police station? Do you want a minute to freshen up, Denae?"

Such a polite way to say she looked a mess between the rumpled clothing, messy hair, and face blotchy from crying. Trevor couldn't help a soft smile. Yet still the most beautiful woman he'd ever known.

Denae swept her hands down her baggy sweatshirt. "Not a bad idea. Then let's walk over. It's such a lovely day. It seems a pity to waste it."

That's my girl.

Who needed an alpha hero? Not Denae. Not when she had this amazing man beside her, fingers entwined firmly with hers, silently supporting her while she gave her statement to the police. This was the kind of man she'd longed for. Not one trying to step in and do things she could or needed to do herself, but right here, ready. She felt safe, protected, *loved* for the first time in her life.

He guided her to a seat in an alcove after she'd answered all their questions, his eyebrows raised in a question of his own. Was she okay? She gave a quick nod and sent him a fleeting smile. She was all right now. Now with Mark behind bars, Mom safe, and Trevor beside her.

She tried to block out her mother's low voice as she laid out the history of her relationship with Mark. Some things Denae didn't want to know.

Pastor Roland settled into the chair on the other side of her. "I didn't know your mother had a degree in counseling."

She let out a short laugh. "Ironic, isn't it?"

"Maybe a Godsend."

Trevor's arm slid around her shoulder as he leaned to see Roland. "What do you mean?"

The pastor looked between them. "Is she thinking of staying in Saddle Springs, do you know? If Mark is behind bars?"

Denae thought about that. "I'm not sure. I imagine she'll go back to Cannon Beach. Jordan is graduating from high school in a few weeks, and Blake is just a year behind. They might be half grown, but they still need a parent around and, with any luck at all, it won't be Mark."

"Not luck, Denae. An answer to prayer, which we've only begun to ask the Lord for. It sounds like Mark will stand trial here for attempted breaking and entering, then be sent back to Oregon for domestic violence charges. If the justice system prevails as it's designed to, he'll be locked up for a few years."

Denae nodded. It would be a relief, and maybe her brothers weren't beyond redemption yet. Maybe the outcome of their dad's situation would point them to the straight and narrow. She could only hope... no, pray. She hadn't really prayed for Jordan or Blake much. They'd been a trial she'd had to endure, and she'd never tried to establish a relationship with them or befriend them. After all, they were so much younger she'd babysat them in her teen years.

"If you think she might be interested, I'd like to talk to her about coming on the team at the women's shelter when it's up and running. We're a few months away yet. Maybe the better part of a year. But someone with her experience on both sides of the equation would be a tremendous asset to the women coming through our doors."

Denae tipped her head and regarded the pastor. She hadn't thought much about how the program would run, only that it was needed and she could help raise funds. "Talk to her about the possibility?"

"I wanted to see how you felt about it first."

"You mean about having her live nearby?"

Pastor Roland nodded.

"It might be good." Denae chewed her lip, thinking.

"We've never been close. I've resented her, despised her, avoided her. To both of our detriment, I think."

Trevor's hand lightly rubbed her shoulder. She leaned back against him, just slightly.

"I was up at the Flying Horseshoe quite a bit last week," Roland went on. "Participating in some of the sessions during the pastoral retreat. I talked to Lisa a few times when she was serving the group."

Huh. Mom hadn't mentioned it.

"She's been thinking through a lot of things since she arrived here. I know she wants to talk to you about them."

A heart-to-heart was likely long overdue. Denae needed to give her the benefit of the doubt.

Mom approached the alcove. "I've asked to see Mark. Do you want to come with me?"

Denae took a long breath. "Do you want me to? I don't particularly want to, but if you need me..."

The pastor stood. "Bonnie and I will be happy to accompany you if you'd like."

Mom's shoulders slacked. "I'd really appreciate that. I don't want to drag Denae through this. There's no need. But it would be nice to have support."

"I can." She didn't want to.

"No, this is probably better." Mom grimaced as Bonnie stepped up on her other side. "But so you know what's going on, I'm filing for divorce. And if he isn't sent to jail, there'll at least be a restraining order. I stayed this long for Jordan's and Blake's sakes, but it might have been a mistake." She straightened her shoulders. "It's not too late for the boys, though. It will do them both good to see the consequences of their father's choices. The way their lives will end up if they keep going the way they are."

Denae jumped to her feet and gave her mom a big squeeze. "I'm so proud of you."

"Oh, sweetie." Mom's voice broke. "You shouldn't be. I didn't stand up for you. I'm so sorry."

"I'm okay." Now. "We'll build from here."

The officer took a few steps over from the desk.

"You go on and see Mark. Trevor and I will wait right here. Then we'll go back to my place together. Stay strong."

"I will." She held her head high and followed the officer, flanked by Roland and Bonnie.

Trevor slid both arms around Denae from behind, his breath warm on her neck. "You're amazing."

She clutched his hands. "I'm not."

"You are," he insisted. "You're strong and brave and a power to be reckoned with."

"No..."

He turned her in his arms and looked deep into her eyes. "You are. You can do anything you set your mind to, from sheer force of will. You've taken this old cowboy, burned by lo—" His voice cut off in mid-word.

"Burned by love?" Denae's eyebrows shot up. "Why, Trevor Delgado, I think you have a story you forgot to tell me."

"Not everything's a story," he said gruffly.

She pushed against his forearms. "If that's how you're going to be about it..."

"Fine." He rolled his eyes. "I thought I was in love a

few years back. It was a mistake, and nothing ever came of it. Ancient history that affects nothing."

Denae tipped her head to one side. "Anyone I know?"

He groaned. "We don't need to talk about it."

"I think we do. Because I want to know everything about you." She walked her fingers up his arms, across the collar of his denim shirt, and onto his unshaved cheeks. "Everything."

Trevor gathered her close. "Okay, whatever. I thought I was in love with Meg Carmichael. Back in her wild days before she got pregnant with Aiden. Before she met Eli."

"Am I anything like Meg?"

His gaze pierced hers. "Not at all, other than both being female. I was young and stupid and tempted by a flirty smile."

Denae waggled her eyebrows and gave him a coy grin. "Like this?"

And Trevor kissed that smirk right off her face.

CHAPTER 22

H ey, bro." Kade stood in his doorway in sweats and bare feet, lamplight puddling out around him. Looking contentedly domesticated. "What's up?"

In the background, Jericho yelled, "Giddyap!" and Harmony laughed, a deep chortle that brought a full smile to Trevor's face. He lifted both hands, each holding a violin case. "I've got something to talk to you about if you have a minute."

Kade's gaze sharpened on the cases then searched Trevor's face. "Sure. Come on in."

"How's Cheri?"

His brother chuckled and stepped aside. "She must be getting close. She baked something like forty dozen cookies today and now she's scrubbing bathrooms. I did the bathrooms yesterday, and I'm pretty sure I did them right, so it's nervous energy, I think."

Trevor set the cases on the table and pushed the smaller one toward his brother. "Remember this?"

Kade unsnapped the latches and lifted out the 1/2-size instrument. "This was yours. Sawyer broke the bow... but it looks fine."

"I bought a new bow for it."

"When? I don't remember ever seeing it since."

"Last week."

His brother's eyebrows rose into his tousled hair.

"I don't know if Jericho or Harmony are interested in learning to play, but I thought I'd offer to loan it to you for a few years if that's a possibility. Learning to play an instrument is important. It exercises a part of your mind that doesn't easily get used any other way."

Kade touched the strings with what looked like reverence. "I was always jealous of you."

"Come again? Because my memory is that you were always too busy being cute to care about stuff like this."

"You were so good at it, and I hated coming in second fiddle to you." He laughed. "Pun intended, I guess."

"Jealous?" Trevor stared at his brother. He must be hearing words that weren't there.

"Yeah. Any idea what it was like being your kid brother? You were a hard act to follow."

He rocked back on his heels. "You're kidding me, right? You did everything perfectly. You charmed the socks off everyone. I spent my childhood in your shadow, wishing I could be as cool as you."

Kade shook his head. "My memories are completely different." He nestled the instrument back into the padded case.

"It's why I quit violin after Sawyer broke my bow,"

Trevor said quietly. "Because it set me apart, and I didn't think it was in a good way."

"Man, I'm sorry." Kade gave him a quick side-hug. "I'll watch for that kind of thing between my kids. I can't believe we were both jealous of each other. That's dumb."

Trevor's heart lifted a little. "Yeah, you're right. Thankfully, I got over myself. Took a long time, though."

Kade unsnapped the second case. "Curiosity is killing me, bro. Because this thing looks shiny and new."

"It is." Trevor lifted the maple instrument from its nest. "This was my birthday present to myself."

"Nice! I had no idea."

"Perks of me living by myself. No one needs to know anything."

"Aw, man..."

Trevor grinned as he adjusted the strings then raised both violin and bow. He waggled his eyebrows and launched into *Ode to Joy*.

Joyful, joyful, we adore You, God of glory, Lord of love; hearts unfold like flowers before You, opening to the sun above. Melt the clouds of sin and sadness; drive the dark of doubt away; giver of immortal gladness, fill us with the light of day!

"Dude! That's seriously awesome."

"You should hear it with Garret's piano behind it."

"No *way*."

"Yes way. I'm..." He took a deep breath. "I'm playing in the talent show."

Kade thumped his back so hard he stumbled.

"Dude, have a care. This baby cost a pretty penny."

"Unca Twevuh! Was that you?" Jericho skidded into the room with his sister on his heels.

Kade crouched. "Uncle Trevor has been practicing and surprised us all. Didn't that sound fantastic?"

Jericho nodded, his eyes bright. "Good job Unca Twevuh!"

"Thanks, bucko. Glad you liked it." Trevor's gaze slid to Harmony.

The seven-year-old had noticed the small violin on the table. She reached out to touch it, but pulled her hand back before she did, her eyes turning up to meet his. Was that longing shining in them?

Trevor exchanged a glance with his brother, who nodded. "That was my violin when I was a little kid about your age, Harmony. I brought it over so your mom and dad could decide if you two could learn to play."

"Really?" Harmony whispered on a breath. "It's so beautiful."

Kade scooped her into his arms. "We'll definitely do what we can, sweet thing, once we get settled in after your baby brother."

Her face fell. "But that's so long."

Kade chuckled. "Not anymore. You'll see. We have to arrange for lessons." He glanced at Trevor. "Who's teaching these days?"

"I'm not sure. So far, I'm learning off YouTube."

"Figures." Kade set Harmony down. "Play another one. I'm impressed at how quickly you picked that back up. Makes me wish I could learn along with the kids."

"Seriously?"

"Yeah. I love music. Always have."

"Well, I so happen to have a solution for you. Dad and Mom gave me Great Grandpa Donovan's violin a few weeks ago. They didn't know I'd already bought my own and I, uh, didn't tell them."

"So you have two?" Kade's gaze sharpened in interest. "Three with the kid-size one?"

"I do. And Donovan was your ancestor as much as he was mine, so you can have his if you want it. It's got beautiful tone, but I'm kind of partial to the new one."

"That'd be awesome. Maybe one day I'll be good enough to do duets with you, but it will take a ton of practice." A grin quirked one side of Kade's mouth. "Although maybe we could start by singing together?"

Trevor chuckled. "You know, that's a possibility. Even for the talent show. It's not too late for an entry." He happened to have an in.

"Rock of Ages?"

He winced. "Anything but that."

"You're here!" Denae gave her best friend a tight hug two weeks later. "I can't believe it. Welcome to Saddle Springs. And you, too, Peter." She offered him a hand, but he gave her a side hug instead.

"Good to see you, Denae."

She turned back to Sadie. "You look amazing. How much weight have you lost?"

Sadie beamed. "The number's not important, but a lot. The important thing is how much better I feel. How much energy I have."

"I'm so excited for you!"

"She can even hike up and down the hill in Bridgeview," Peter bragged with a laugh. "I can hardly keep up with her."

Sadie's elbow found her husband's ribs. "That's not true, and you know it."

"I know nothing of the sort. You'd be proud of her, Denae. She's even taken up basketball."

"No way."

Sadie rolled her eyes. "And I'm terrible at it. I've played with the guys maybe ten times now, and I almost got a basket once."

"The ball went around the rim twice then fell off the outside of it," Peter said. "She'll get the next one."

Denae laughed. They were too adorable, and Peter's support seemed unwavering. Sadie seemed to have come to grips with her insecurities of a couple of months ago.

Sadie looked her up and down. "How about you, girl? I've been so worried about you."

Wow, that was going to be a long story. "Come on in. Let's not stand on the doorstep all evening."

"I'll grab our luggage." Peter turned for the car at the curb as Sadie followed Denae inside.

"Cute place." Sadie looked around.

"So tiny." Denae sighed. "But it's not bad, I guess."

"Maybe you won't be here much longer? Mr. Hunky Cowboy and all."

"Maybe."

"How's it going, being out at Standing Rock?"

Denae had told Sadie about her reaction. Over-reaction. "I've discussed it with my therapist in Missoula.

Prayed about it with Pastor Roland. Walked the arena with Trevor." She took a deep breath. "It's getting better. Good memories are replacing the dark ones."

"That's great." Sadie hugged her. "You've made so much progress."

"There's such a long way to go. I feel like I need to improve myself before being with Trevor is a real possibility, though. I'm still not good enough."

Sadie swept both hands down her sides. There had to be a hundred pounds gone in the past two years. "Not necessarily. Peter fell in love with a very imperfect me. And you know something? I'm kind of glad about that."

"I'm not following."

"He already knows I'm not perfect. I'm a work-in-progress, and so is he. We're under no illusions."

Huh. Her friend had a point. Trevor certainly knew the good, the bad, and the ugly about her. She'd seen his sulky, hurting side, too. But both of them admitted it and were working and praying through the issues.

Peter appeared at the door dragging two carry-ons. "Where shall I put these?"

"Follow me. My guest room is upstairs at the front of the house, and there's even a small bath off the hallway." Denae led the way.

Peter deposited the luggage on the chest under the window, but Sadie glanced the other way. "Ooh, this is where the magic happens." She headed into Denae's office and stopped. "Why don't you use your desk like a normal person?"

The desk straddling the treadmill held her open laptop along with a stack of papers, a pen holder, and other paraphernalia, while the official walnut desk held a blotter with February's calendar on top. In May. It was kind of obvious which she considered her real workspace. "I like to keep in shape?" But the words faded from her lips.

Sadie shook her head. "We've talked about this."

"I know." Denae winced. "It was a rough winter, but things are looking up. Honest."

"What does Mr. Hunky Cowboy have to say about all this?"

"He knows. And he seems to love me anyway."

Sadie stepped closer and gently tapped Denae's breastbone. "If he loves you, it's not *because* you are skinny. He loves you in spite of it."

"You're right." Denae squeezed her friend. "I can't wait for you to meet him. In fact, it's not too early to drive up to Standing Rock. I want you to see the place I disappeared to when I left Cannon Beach every summer. And meet Larkspur, too." The poor gelding had only spent a few days at Canyon Crossing before Trevor had hauled him back to Standing Rock.

"But mostly the cowboy."

"Well, duh, girlfriend." She jabbed Sadie in the ribs. "Of course. You guys need a few minutes to freshen up? I'll finish prepping the salad I'm taking up for dinner."

Sadie's eyebrows rose. "Don't tell me the cowboy exists on rabbit food."

"Nope. Trust me, there will be steak and grilled asparagus as well."

"And you'll eat those things?"

Denae took a deep breath. "Some, yeah. I'm working on it, girl. I really am."

"Well, Peter did some sugar-free baking last night. I hope to entice you to try some of that."

"Fudge and strawberry cheesecake," came Peter's voice from behind her. "Approved by everyone, even my nonna."

Sadie tucked her hand around Denae's arm. "Well, I'm ready to meet this paragon of yours. Let's go."

RANGER AND MICKEY warned Trevor that Denae and her friends had arrived. What would they think of him? He looked down at his grilling apron. Off or on? No, he was done worrying about stupid stuff like that. He strode to the front door and swung it wide.

Denae stepped forward and pecked his lips then turned to perform the introductions.

Trevor tucked her against his left side and reached out to shake first Sadie's hand then Peter's. "Welcome to Standing Rock."

"Good to be here." Peter's grip was stronger than expected... for a city boy. But he had an active job, if Trevor remembered correctly. "It's all much bigger than I expected. How many acres?"

"My family ranches about eighty thousand acres."

The other guy's eyes widened. "Wow. That's... a lot."

Trevor nodded. "I guess. Eaglecrest Ranch up the road has been in our family for a few generations, and my parents still live there, hopefully for a long time to come.

We bought this spread a few years ago from Denae's dad and stepmom. And my brother and sister-in-law own a fair chunk of benchland along the river across the road. Her grandparents live there, also."

"All in the family, eh?" Peter grinned.

"My kid brother rides rodeo. Maybe someday he'll grow up and take some responsibility around here, but I'm not holding my breath. Anyway, come on in, unless you want the grand tour first?"

"Man, could we? I'd love to see the place." Peter glanced around.

Denae pulled away and hooked her arm through Sadie's. "Come on and meet Larkspur. Trevor and I were wondering if you guys would like to go for a trail ride tomorrow?"

"Oh, I don't know..." Sadie grimaced. "Horses are so tall, and I—"

"And you are courageous and up for new experiences," Denae interrupted. "That's one of the things I love most about you."

"Um..." Sadie cast an entreaty over her shoulder at her husband.

He only grinned at her. "Me too, Denae. She's a brave one."

"I am *not*!"

"Well, sweetheart, I've never been on a horse in my life, either, but I think it would be fun to give it a try."

Sadie rolled her eyes as Denae towed her toward the stable, Ranger and Mickey prancing around them.

"They're quite a pair," Peter said with a laugh. "Did Denae ever tell you how she and I met on the phone?"

"No, I don't think so."

He chuckled. "Ask her sometime. She's a force to be reckoned with, that one. She's been a solid friend for Sadie, even long distance, and I'm very thankful for her."

Trevor eyed the other man. Somehow he hadn't realized Denae's friendship with Sadie extended to Peter, but he should have guessed. Her bubbly personality wouldn't leave anyone on the sidelines. Even an old grump like him. "You're right about that."

"She's come a long way in the past year."

The stable door stood ajar. From the dim depths, he heard Sadie's squeal, hopefully of delight. Either way, it was his stable and his responsibility, so he headed over there with Peter at his side. He stopped at the sight of Sadie offering a piece of apple to Larkspur with a wide grin on her face.

Peter chuckled. "I guess the trail ride will be a go."

CHAPTER 23

Trevor nodded at Garret then heard the intro pour from his friend's hands. It was too late to back out now. He stood on the stage of the Saddle Springs Community Center, blinded by the spotlights, barely able to see into the crowd, which was just as well. Hundreds of people filled the auditorium. Everyone he knew. Everyone who knew him.

He swallowed hard, tucked the violin under his chin, and lifted the bow.

Joyful, joyful, we adore You, God of glory, Lord of love; hearts unfold like flowers before You, opening to the sun above. Melt the clouds of sin and sadness; drive the dark of doubt away; giver of immortal gladness, fill us with the light of day!

So much for the haunting melody of *Ashokan Farewell.* It was a beautiful piece, but not for today. Not when his heart was full of wonder.

Trevor kept an eye on Garret at the grand piano, watching for his cues. The music burst into the final stanza, and Trevor's bow and heart soared with it. He'd denied his dreams of playing for far too long, and what good was a talent if it was kept hidden in the confines of his own home?

There was silence for two solid seconds after the final notes drifted away, then the audience surged to their feet and the applause began.

It felt better than he'd imagined.

Clapping, Denae came in from the wings, her eyes shining as she approached the mic. "Give it up for our own Trevor Delgado!"

"*Your* own, you mean!" some wise guy hollered from the crowd.

She lifted the mic off the stand. "It works for me."

A few guys whistled along with the laughter.

Trevor just stood there, instrument tucked under his arm, grinning like a fool, and waited for Kade to join him onstage.

Denae's gaze locked with his as she spoke into the mic. "There's been a slight change in our lineup tonight. The next number, as noted in your program, was to be a duet from the Delgado brothers."

Was? Unease knotted Trevor's gut.

"However, I've just heard that Kade and Cheri entered the maternity ward at Mustang County Hospital a few minutes ago. Labor is well under way. Strangely, that means Kade isn't here to sing. So, unless Trevor wants to sing a solo...?"

He shook his head and took a step back. Probably looked like a feral horse cornered in a box pen.

Laughter rippled across the auditorium.

Denae turned toward the front. "Then we'll move

into the final number, a musical medley presented by James Carmichael and Garret Morrison. We hope you'll join us downstairs to wrap up the bake sale and silent auction." She paused, hands clenched around the mic. "I can't thank you enough for this generous outpouring of support for the safe house. We've raised a significant portion of our budget with this event. Thank you." She nodded at James and Garret and headed offstage.

Trevor followed her into the ready room. He set the violin in its open case and turned for her. "Kade phoned you?"

She shook her head, eyes shining, as she stepped into his arms. "He called your mom, and she came and found me. I imagine they're heading over to the hospital to wait. That baby was due two weeks ago. Who ever thought he'd be born in the middle of our talent show?"

Trevor chuckled. "The Delgado way, I suppose. Always seeking the spotlight." He bent and caressed her lips with his own.

Denae nestled against him. "Don't get a swelled head just because you were the surprise hit of the evening, buddy. You might need a bigger cowboy hat."

"I could use a new one." He lifted his Stetson off and set it on her head. "This one fits you just fine. Cowgirl."

"I've been called worse."

"Have you, now? Let me give you some names." He tipped the hat back on her head and kissed her. "Beautiful." He kissed her again, punctuating each title with another. "Charming. Victorious. Dreamer. Winner."

"What did I win?" she whispered.

"Me." He looked deeply into the windows of her soul. "If you'll accept the prize."

She fingered the collar of his denim shirt and glanced coyly at him. "I'm not sure what you're saying, Mr. Delgado."

"That's Mr. Hunky Cowboy to you, Ms. Archibald."

Her face pinked. "You overheard Sadie."

"I did. But I didn't hear you arguing."

"Your head's definitely swelling. And I still didn't hear a question, exactly."

He tugged a tiny box out of his jeans pocket. "You mean the question that might go with something like this?"

Denae's eyes widened and her hands flew to cover her mouth.

Trevor dropped on one knee and popped the box open. "Denae, I love you. Would you do me the honor of becoming my wife?"

"Seriously, Trevor?" she squealed. "Here? Now?"

"I thought we'd wait a few months for the wedding, but if you want here and now, we might be able to arrange it. Pastor Roland is in the audience." He looked up at her, a tinge of worry suddenly fluttering. Had he misread her? Didn't she love him as he loved her? How could he breathe if she didn't?

"Trevor." She put her hands on either side of his cheeks and kissed him so thoroughly he nearly lost his balance. "I love you."

Which wasn't quite an answer. He held his position, gut churning.

"You're the one doing me the honor," she whispered. "I want to marry you."

He slipped the princess-cut diamond onto her finger and surged to his feet, gathering her close and removing his hat from her head so he could kiss her properly.

Applause flooded the auditorium.

"Do you need to go back out there?" he murmured against her lips. "I thought we'd have more time." He thought she'd say yes more quickly.

She shook her head and pulled his shirt collar closer. "Kiss me, cowboy."

Gladly.

THE SILENT AUCTION area looked busy when Denae, feeling disheveled, pulled Trevor into it a few minutes later. Amanda Carmichael tugged a pen out of Wyatt Torrington's hand and scrawled a bid on a piece of paper offering a side of beef. Wyatt snatched it back and wrote another, eyebrows cocked at Amanda to the laughter of those surrounding them. The best kind of bidding war was under way.

Across the room, Sadie and Peter stood with Dad and Michelle, each with a glass of wine in hand. "Ready?" Denae asked, glancing up at Trevor.

The expression in his gorgeous eyes warmed her to the core. "So very, very ready." He slipped his arm around her, drawing her close. "Fair warning. Your dad might not seem particularly surprised."

Denae whirled to face him. "You asked my *dad?*"

"Isn't that what a guy is supposed to do? I flipped to the back of a couple of Cheri's romance novels and double-checked."

She bit her lip, trying to hold back giggles.

"Don't tell me I got it wrong. That's where the whole down-on-one-knee thing came from, too. Was that a waste? Because it's sure uncomfortable down there while the girl takes her sweet time coming up with an affirmative answer."

"You didn't."

"I absolutely did. You might know how it's supposed to be done, but I had no clue. And I didn't dare ask Kade. He would've only made fun of me. He's done it like three times now. Total pro."

"Oh, Trevor." She slipped her arms up around his neck, right there in the middle of everything, and kissed him.

"Yo, *girl*!" called Sadie. "What's that I see on your hand?"

Trevor nuzzled into Denae's neck. "Guess the cat's out of the bag now."

"Guess so," she whispered against his ear. "Oh, well."

He chuckled and turned away, raising her left hand high. "She said yes!"

Screams and squeals filled the air as their friends crowded around. Somehow she became separated from Trevor as James, Garret, and others surrounded him. She was squeezed from one side then the other until she felt like she'd been caught in a pinball machine.

Dad pulled her out of the melee. "I'm happy for you, honey. He's a good guy."

"The best, Daddy. I can't believe it."

"A bit extreme as a way to move back into Standing Rock, I've got to say." Dad's eyes twinkled. "But, hey, whatever works."

Michelle batted Dad's arm then moved in for a hug. "Good for you, sweetie. Just turn me loose if you want help with wedding plans. Or not. Your call."

Denae blinked. "I have no idea. This is all so sudden, and we haven't talked about a date or anything." Unless Trevor meant it about here and now. No, that wasn't the romantic way to do it. She'd always wanted the big church wedding with all the traditions. She'd do it right. The time would go quickly.

Dad kissed Michelle's cheek. "Denae might want her mother involved. Glad Lisa finally ditched that loser, is all I can say."

Michelle rolled her eyes. "Well, if Denae wants someone with good taste, she knows where to find her. I promise to play nice."

Denae giggled. "Thanks, Michelle. I can't tell you how much I appreciate you. I'll find ways to keep you and my mom both in the loop." Might be a challenge.

"There's someone else here to see you, sweetie." Her stepmom pointed toward the photo exhibits across the room. "I was just talking to that lovely young woman over there."

"Marissa!" Denae shrieked, dodging through the crowd to fling herself at the dark-haired beauty. "I can't believe you came." After a quick hug, she pulled herself together and smoothed her dress before offering her hand to the redheaded man beside Marissa. "Hi, Jase."

Marissa Mackie, the coordinator of the Miss Snowflake Pageant, offered a megawatt smile. "I always love to keep up with what our protégées are doing." She indicated Denae's photo display behind her. "You made such a big difference at the pageant, drawing awareness to eating disorders. It's a lasting legacy, and the foundation you built has given me some tools for working with our contestants. So many have suffered while trying to meet society's standard of beauty."

Pink shame clung to Denae's cheeks. "I haven't done so well myself."

"But you're overcoming. Aren't you?"

Denae straightened. "I am. With Jesus' help and the love of a good man."

Marissa slipped her hand into Jase's. "Jesus is enough, but having a good guy at our sides? The best bonus in the business."

"I want you to meet Trevor. He's amazing."

Marissa and Jase exchanged a smile.

Denae searched the crowd for her beloved only to find him coming toward her with a cell phone stuck to one ear while he blocked the din with his other hand. He gave her a grin but remained focused on the call. Then he tucked the phone in his pocket.

"Donovan Delgado made his appearance about twenty minutes ago." Trevor snugged Denae close to his side. "All is well."

CHAPTER 24

So many people had gathered on Trevor's back patio. He should be panicked out about invasions on his space, or about being a good host, or about how such a diverse crew would get along. Michelle and Stewy chatted with Trevor's mom by the rose gardens while Lisa visited with Pastor Roland and Bonnie way across the patio, her back to her ex and his wife.

Hey, it was Mom's party. She'd simply decided Standing Rock was the better venue to celebrate the safe house, her son's engagement, and the birth of her newest grandson.

Denae curled in Trevor's lap in the oversize Adirondack chair, arms around his neck, ignoring both her parents. Ignoring everyone, actually, and he was happy to play along. He held her close, sneaking kisses, but keeping an eye on the group.

"Unca Twevuh? I gots a new brother." Jericho clambered up into the chair, elbowing Denae for a little space as he grabbed Trevor's cheeks between two pudgy hands.

Trevor grinned and gathered his nephew close with one arm. "You sure do, bucko. You'll have a lot of fun playing with him."

Jericho's nose curled. "He too little. He sleep and cry."

"He'll get bigger. Did you know your daddy was my baby brother, and I was the big brother like you?"

"Really?"

"Yes, really." Trevor caught sight of Kade striding toward them with Harmony on his shoulders. He raised his voice. "Your daddy slept and cried a lot, too. And he was *so* stinky."

Kade dropped into the chair beside Trevor as he swung Harmony to the brick patio. "What nonsense are you filling Jer's head with now?"

"Just the truth." Trevor smirked. "Us big brothers like me'n Jer have to stick together. I'll teach him how to treat a little brother."

"Sounds like a threat." Kade sighed, but a grin softened his face. "You're a pretty decent big brother, so Jer could learn from worse."

"Aw, thanks. Don't hold back the praise."

Kade settled deep into the chair and closed his eyes, Harmony snuggled against him.

For once, Trevor could see his brother as a dad without envy. It would happen for him, too. He pressed a kiss to Denae's temple. "When would you like to get married?"

She pulled back a little and looked into his eyes. "I always thought I'd like a June wedding." She nibbled on her lip with a worried expression.

"It's nearly the end of May. Sounds like a tight deadline, but I'm sure we can manage."

Kade snorted, but his eyes remained shut.

Denae shook her head. "It takes longer than that."

"All we need is a marriage license and a preacher. The rest is trappings..." Even as he said the words, Trevor knew. Denae was a romantic through and through. Those trappings meant a lot to her. He gulped. "A whole year?"

"You should have proposed at Christmas." Kade chuckled.

"Not your conversation, man." Trevor jabbed his brother with his elbow. "Besides, we weren't even dating at Christmas."

"You brought up the topic with me sitting right here. Not my fault."

"When's Cheri coming home with the baby? She usually keeps you in line."

"Probably in the morning. Donovan's a little jaundiced so they wanted to keep an eye for another day. I'm headed down to see them in a bit."

"So you'd better get a decent night's sleep while you can."

Kade opened one eye and squinted at him. "Your turn will come, bro. Then we'll see who's laughing."

Denae nestled her head against Trevor's shoulder, but Jericho squirmed to get down. Harmony joined her brother as they ran off to play with Juliana and Aiden. Trevor didn't even care that Meg and Eli had come to the party. She was so far in the rearview mirror their brief relationship might as well never have happened. Not much had, anyway. Most of it had been in Trevor's imagination.

Trevor snuggled Denae close, kissing her hair. "How about a Christmas wedding?" Surely seven months was more than enough.

Kade snorted.

"But then we couldn't have a reception out here on the patio, and the roses wouldn't be in bloom."

"So… June. A whole year?" An entire eternity, really.

"Have pity on him, Denae," said Kade. "He'll be thirty-three by then. One foot in the grave."

Trevor glared at him. "Don't you have somewhere else you need to be? Some other conversation you need to hijack?"

"I don't think so. This is quite entertaining." Kade smirked. "It's not every day I get to hassle my bro without repercussions. He's usually not this mellow."

"I'll mellow you."

"Terrified, bro. Shaking in my boots."

Denae giggled as she pushed out of his embrace. "You two are something else. I think I'll go talk to Sadie while you finish insulting each other."

"We'll never be done," Kade warned. "And, uh, welcome to the family. Cheri was excited when I told her the news this morning."

"I can't wait to see her in person." Denae twisted the diamond ring, smiling down at it. "And to meet the new little guy. I haven't been around a newborn since my brothers were that size, and I don't remember much."

"You guys can babysit any time you want, you know. Practice up for your turn."

Denae grinned at Kade. "Maybe." Then she sashayed over to where Sadie and Peter stood talking to each other.

"Mom showed me her video of your violin solo last night. Good job, bro."

"She took one?" Trevor turned to his brother. "I thought they'd gone to the hospital right away."

Kade punched his arm lightly. "Are you kidding me? They were there for you. Dad was popping his buttons with pride. Sorry I stood you up, though."

"We can sing that one some Sunday morning in church. Any time. You were definitely needed elsewhere."

"That woman of yours is amazing."

"Yeah… but why do you say so?"

"Look at you, all out of your shell and everything. I've always loved you, bro, but I'm liking this version even more."

Trevor chuckled. "Yeah, blame everything on Denae." And God.

"Carmen, I'd like you to meet my friends Sadie and Peter from Spokane. Sadie and I were best friends growing up in Oregon."

"Pleased to meet you." Carmen smiled warmly as she shook their hands. "I'm sure you know what a solid, loyal friend Denae is."

A flush crept up Denae's cheeks at Carmen's words and Sadie's answering smile.

"She really is. She certainly had my back since we were kids, and I wish we still lived in the same town."

Denae laughed. "You're the one who insisted on passing the bar in Washington not Montana."

"You're the one who insisted on moving to Cowboyville instead of Spokane, even though you can work from anywhere in the world."

Denae's gaze caught on Trevor's across the patio. He winked at her then turned back to whatever his brother was saying. She couldn't help the grin that suffused her face. "I think I made the right decision, frankly. Saddle Springs is the exact right place for me."

"I, for one, am sure glad you moved here." Carmen draped an arm over Denae's shoulders. "I needed an understanding friend as much as Trevor and Standing Rock need you. This place is so big. It really needs a bunch of kids one day."

"Maybe." Denae could hardly wait to hold baby Donovan. Did she really want to wait an entire year to marry Trevor? Donovan would be at least two years old before he had a little cousin at that rate. It didn't need to be today's decision.

"Here comes Mr. Hunky Cowboy," Sadie whispered.

Peter laughed, shaking his head at his wife's drama.

Denae turned to see Trevor sauntering toward them, his face lit with an inner glow that hadn't been there a year ago. His cowboy boots clinked on the patio bricks. His denim shirt tucked into blue jeans, only divided by a leather belt with a brass buckle. He was softer, gentler, yet even more masculine than ever.

Her heart lifted in response as he set his cowboy hat on her head before bending down and kissing her.

Her cowboy. Her dream come true.

ACKNOWLEDGMENTS

If you've read previous stories of mine, you'll know that cowboy romance is a minor variation on my usual themes of farm-and-garden such as in my flagship Farm Fresh Romance series. The Montana Ranches overlap slightly with both the Garden Grown Romances (part of the multi-author Arcadia Valley Romance series) where Cheri (Mackenzie) Delgado played a small role, and with the Urban Farm Fresh Romance series, where Denae Archibald appears as a friend to Sadie Guthrie in *Raindrops on Radishes*.

Thanks to Elizabeth Maddrey for being Chief Prodder and First Reader as well as a terrific author whose stories I enjoy reading!

I also appreciate my beta readers: Paula, Amy, Joelle, Gretchen, and Lynnette. Thanks for loving this new direction, encouraging me, and catching my errors... although I'm sure I managed to leave a few in, even after my fabulous editor, Nicole, had her input. Thanks for sticking with me through all these years and stories, Nicole.

I'm also grateful for the Christian Indie Authors Facebook group and my sister bloggers at Inspy Romance. These folks make a difference in my life every single day. I'm thrilled to walk beside them as we tell stories for Jesus!

Thank you to my Facebook friends, followers, street team, and reader group members for prayers, encouragement, and great fellowship. If you'd like to join other readers who love my stories, please find us at Valerie Comer: Readers Group.

Thanks to my husband, Jim, whose love for me never fails and who encourages me in every endeavor. Thanks to my kids, their spouses, and my wonderful grandgirls for cheering me on. To them, having an author for a mom/grandma is "normal." Imagine that!

All my love and gratitude goes to Jesus, the One who is my vision, the High King of Heaven, the lord of my heart. Thank you. A thousand times, thank you.

Montana
Ranches
Christian Romance Series

THE
COWBOY'S
Convenient Marriage

SADDLE SPRINGS ROMANCE - BOOK 4

USA Today Bestselling Author
VALERIE COMER

Spencer Haviland had prided himself on planning his life to the tiniest detail. Until two days ago.

Now he turned off the ignition and stared at the unassuming low-slung house in front of him, its weathered clapboards sagging as though becoming one with nature. In fact, the entire ranch surrounding him looked too exhausted to carry on.

What had he been thinking?

No second guessing. He'd made the only choice that made sense on Saturday night, loading all his personal effects into his sports car and heading northwest... but the Rocking H of his childhood memories and the Rocking H of today bore little resemblance to each other.

The decision was *still* the only thing that made sense. It was just going to be more work than he'd anticipated. Take longer. Well, he had nothing but time.

Spencer winced at the thought as he swung his long legs out of the Maserati into the blistering August heat.

The lazy aroma of drying hay wafted on the slight flutter of air tickling the sweat already beading on his face. Bees buzzed amidst the weeds strangling the porch steps.

His memories zinged, too. Memories of visiting the ranch with his grandfather and chasing his second cousin around on horseback. Eric had been older and spent a lot of time on the ranch, always eager to show off to the visitor. In the end, Eric's recklessness had killed him.

A creak pulled his attention to the plank door, now slightly ajar. "Spencer, is that you? Now you're a sight for sore eyes."

Two Border collies bounded across the sparse grass then dropped to a crouch just out of reach and eyed him eagerly. Keeping the dogs in his line of vision, Spencer climbed the three steps and held out his hand. "Uncle Howard?"

The old man shifted a few steps back, looking Spencer over from head to toe.

Spencer returned the favor. His great-uncle's bushy white hair and eyebrows crowned faded blue eyes. Jeans and a plaid shirt that had seen better days draped from his lean body. Spencer's gaze drifted to the old man's feet. The boots looked so battered they might've been the same pair he'd worn during Spencer's childhood.

"Well, it's good to see you, boy. Got some working clothes along, I hope?" The old man clapped him on the shoulder, nearly knocking him flying.

Spencer glanced down at his trouser shorts, perfect for Friday afternoons at the golf club. Those days were behind him. "Yes, I've got jeans." Not Levi's, but something much trendier and probably less durable. He'd adapt.

"Good, good." Uncle Howard's chin indicated Spencer's Toms slip-ons. "Can't ride in them shoes, neither."

He might've lived in Texas most of his life, but he hadn't owned cowboy boots since the last pair his grandfather bought him when he was a kid. On that last trip to Montana, most likely. "I'll get myself a pair in Missoula once we've figured a few things out." He'd need the boots if the attorney's letter had accurately portrayed his new life.

Howard nodded. "Fair enough. We'll make a cowpoke out of you again. C'mon in, boy. Want coffee?"

It wouldn't be Starbucks. He'd have to drive into Missoula for a decent cup, most likely, and that wouldn't happen every day. Well, he'd learn to live with it. "Sure, that'd be great. Can I help?"

His uncle waved toward the rustic table by the wide window. "Have a seat. I'll get it for you."

The kitchen matched the over-all faded feel of the place. The old man crossed the space to an electric stove flanked by chipped cream-painted cabinets and lifted a monster-sized blue enamel coffee pot.

Taking a deep breath, Spencer took a seat on a wooden chair. A moment later, a giant pottery mug of black coffee plunked down, sloshing over onto the table's hand-sawn planks.

Grandpa's voice drifted from Spencer's childhood. "Gonna drink coffee, boy? You gotta drink it like a man." He might even have said it right here at this table.

Likely the brothers had the same upbringing. There would be no offer of hazelnut creamer or even sugar. Spencer eyed the mug. How bad could it be? The aroma clogged his nose. Smelled like the real thing, for sure. On steroids. "Thanks, Uncle Howard."

"So, you came." Howard settled in the curved wooden chair at the table's head and wrapped two gnarled, trembling hands around a cup of his own. "Finally."

Spencer nodded and blew a bit of steam off the top of the mug. "Yes, sir."

"Been a long time."

"It has."

"I wasn't sure about you. Your pa turned you into a city boy. I didn't know if cowboying still flowed through your veins."

Was this where he said he wasn't sure, either? When he'd received the registered letter from Uncle Howard's attorney a month ago, he figured he'd bide his time and claim his inheritance when the old man died then sell the ranch to the highest bidder. He didn't need property in Montana, but cashing it in would enable him to upgrade his Dallas lifestyle a notch or two.

His and Madison's. He'd been ready to propose that night. It had seemed the logical next step, and the party had been planned for exactly that event. But Madison hadn't even caught a glimpse of the little velvet box still wedged in his shorts pocket.

And she never would.

His great-uncle didn't need to know how far removed

the Rocking H was from Spencer's first choice. He picked his words carefully. "I've lived in Dallas all my life, that's true. But I've never forgotten this place and how much I loved coming out in the summers with Grandpa." Did he have what it took to run this place? Yes. There weren't any other acceptable options.

Howard eyed him warily. "Fred says my mind is slipping. He tell you that?"

Spencer nodded. The attorney had said that and a whole lot more when Spencer phoned him this morning from somewhere near the Wyoming border.

"I don't see it myself." Howard scratched his neck. "Though sometimes I don't rightly recall how I got someplace or why Carmen is looking at me strange."

"Must be tough." Grandpa had always said Howard was sharper than a tack.

"Anyway, Fred said it's time to set things in order, while I can still do so with a clear mind." Howard slurped his coffee. "With Eric six feet under, I guess you're the only Haviland left."

As usual, Spencer was the last resort. Would Madison even have said yes if he'd popped the question on one knee? Surely she'd understood the purpose of the gathering of their closest friends and both families. He yanked himself back to the ranch kitchen. "Not the only one. There's Eric's widow and their daughter."

Howard waved his hand. "She's a good girl, Carmen is. She's been trying hard, but it takes a man to run a spread the size of the Rocking H. Most of the hayfields and rangelands are leased out, but it's time to reclaim what belongs to the Haviland name. Why, my grandpa Delbert was one of the first settlers in this area. He staked out the Rocking H round about the time the railway went in, and they were cryin' for beef back east. He built up this side of the valley, and William Delgado took the other."

Delgado. Sounded vaguely familiar.

"Those Delgados think they're something else. They've bought up Standing Rock, and one of their sons married into Paradise Creek Ranch. They're too big for their britches, them Delgados. At least those boys haven't come sniffing around Carmen."

Spencer blinked, trying to catch up. "Why would they?" He wanted nothing to do with a feud over ranch land or grazing rights or whatever the going term was in the twenty-first century.

"She's a pretty girl, Carmen, and a good cook if you like fancy stuff like pizza. But they've missed their chance to get their hands on the Rocking H, now that you're here." Howard smirked at him, slapping the table.

Maybe they'd be interested in buying the ranch when Spencer was ready to sell. He filed the information away then lifted the coffee mug and took a deep slurp, sputtering on the tarry bitterness. There might not be a Starbucks anywhere near the ranch, but surely people could make decent coffee at home. He'd learn how, starting tomorrow, unless Carmen could do a better job than the old man.

He looked around the kitchen, obviously a woman's domain with the gingham curtains and polka-dotted potholders. "Where *is* Carmen?"

"Gone down to Saddle Springs for groceries or some such thing. Cain't rightly recall." Uncle Howard grinned. "Ain't she gonna be surprised to see you here?"

"Mommy! Mommy, look! There's a shiny red car at our house."

Carmen Haviland narrowed her gaze at the expensive-looking sports car. "So there is, sweetie. Looks like Uncle Howard has company. Want to help me carry in the groceries?"

Six-year-old Juliana slumped dramatically into her booster in the SUV's backseat. "Do I *have* to?"

"You sure do." Carmen glared at the Texas license plate. All evidence pointed to the arrival of Eric's second cousin. Her work was cut out for her. She had to make Uncle Howard see that a city boy was unfit to inherit the Rocking H, and that she was a much better choice. If only Howard actually let her make any decisions, he'd soon see how she could turn this place around, but he smiled indulgently, all but patting her on the head like he did Juliana, and that was that.

She handed two of the lighter bags to Juliana and gathered as many more in her own hands as she could, nudging the door shut with her foot. It might be a while before she could get back for the rest, and she didn't want to leave an open invitation to Gwynn or Selah. "Let's go see who's here." She straightened her shoulders and turned to her daughter, only to hear the front door click shut.

No. Who knew what the child would say to Spencer or to Howard?

Carmen jogged up the steps and fumbled with the knob around her bags. She got inside the door in time to hear Juliana's voice.

"My name is Juliana Erica Haviland. Who're you?"

"I'm Spencer, your daddy's cousin."

His voice was deeper than Carmen remembered, but then, she hadn't been paying much attention the last two times they'd met. He'd come for the wedding, and he'd come for Eric's funeral. Both events had been held in the Springs of Living Water Church down in Saddle Springs. Neither time had the man set foot on the Rocking H.

She stepped into the kitchen doorway behind her daughter. "Spencer. What a surprise."

"Carmen, it's good to see you. I hope you're doing well?"

He wore a white golf shirt with a logo on the chest and dressy shorts. And on his feet? Slip-on canvas loafers. Perfect ranch attire, she thought, stifling an eyeroll. And Uncle Howard thought Spencer could do a better job operating the Rocking H than she could?

She'd ignore the fact that he was good-looking. In a completely different way than her husband had been, of course, but it didn't matter what he looked like. Could he ride? Rope? Brand? Because, if he couldn't, he might as well drive that little red car back to Dallas, sooner rather than later.

He stood and extended his hand, blue eyes just like Eric's drilling through her. No humor. No friendliness. Simply assessment.

Carmen raised her chin slightly and set her groceries on the floor. "I'm fine, thank you." She shook his hand with a firm grasp. She was strong. She was capable. She didn't need a city boy here to take what was rightfully hers... or, at least, what was rightfully Juliana's. She'd show him up every step of the way until he conceded her claim and slinked back to Texas.

His eyebrows peaked, and a glint sparked in his eyes.

Oh, sure, *now* he grinned. She'd show him. She'd wipe that smirk off his face. *Later, buster.*

"Mommy, I can't reach the table." Juliana strained with the grocery bag in her hands.

With a final glare at the intruder, Carmen stepped around him and lifted Juliana's load to the table. She turned for her own and rammed straight into a broad, solid chest. Her nostrils filled with a woodsy cologne. "Excuse me."

"Looking for these?" Spencer set the rest of the bags on the table. "Here you go."

"Thanks." Why did the jerk need to be polite? He'd be winning points with Uncle Howard with a chivalrous move like that. He didn't need any more. He needed a failure big enough to lose all the points he had or dreamed of attaining. She wasn't necessarily above helping him find that misstep, either.

Her conscience twitched.

Okay, fine. She wouldn't *make* him do anything stupid. No doubt he was perfectly capable of blundering all by himself. She'd simply be ready to pick up the pieces and make sure Uncle Howard noticed.

That was all.

**The Cowboy's Convenient Marriage
is now available.**

Valerie Comer lives where food meets faith in her real life, her fiction, and on her blog and website. She and her husband of over 35 years farm, garden, and keep bees on a small farm in Western Canada, where they grow and preserve much of their own food.

Valerie has always been interested in real food from scratch, but her conviction has increased dramatically since God blessed her with four delightful granddaughters. In this world of rampant disease and pollution, she is compelled to do what she can to make these little girls' lives the best she can. She helps supply healthy food — local food, organic food, seasonal food — to grow strong bodies and minds.

Valerie is a *USA Today* bestselling author and a two-time Word Award winner. She is known for writing engaging characters, strong communities, and deep faith laced with humor into her green clean romances.

To find out more, visit her website www.valeriecomer.com where you can read her blog, and explore her many links. You can also find Valerie blogging with other authors of Christian contemporary romance at Inspy Romance.

Why not join her email list where you will find news, giveaways, deals, book recommendations, and more? Your thank-you gift is *Promise of Peppermint*, the prequel novella to the Urban Farm Fresh Romance series.

http://valeriecomer.com/subscribe

CPSIA information can be obtained
at www.ICGtesting.com
Printed in the USA
LVHW110903290123
738170LV00005B/79

9 781988 068442